Be careful of howling at the full moon!

James W... (signature)

This one is for my family. My mom, Dave, Uncle Les,
Aunt Helen, Andrea, Peter and Justin.
Simply put, you guys rock.

Published in 2010 by Be Read, an imprint of Simply Read Books
www.simplyreadbooks.com

Text © 2010 by James McCann
Cover and interior images © 2010 by A. Matsoureff

Book Design by Elisa Gutiérrez

CATALOGUING IN PUBLICATION DATA
McCann, J. Alfred (James Alfred)
Rancour / James McCann

ISBN 978-1-897476-11-6 (pbk.).--ISBN 978-1-897476-08-6 (bound)

I. Title.
PS8575.C387R35 2010   jC813'.54   C2010-901192-9

Printed in Canada   10 9 8 7 6 5 4 3 2 1

Canada Council   Conseil des Arts
for the Arts   du Canada

James McCann

Rancour

Be Read

"Man has tried to define good and evil since the dawn of his first sin. It seems to me that with every definition mankind only succeeds in furthering himself from the truth. Even after an eternity of debate the question still remains: Is good and evil a perception of the mind, the result of a single action, or a combination of the two? From my experience this is what I have learned: Mankind spends far too much time philosophizing what evil is, and far too little ending what is corrupted in himself."

-Wulfsign

MINITAW

CEMETARY

BASS AVE

PIKE AVE

WILLOW STREET

MAIN STREET

TROUT AVE

MINNOW AVE

FILLMORE HIGH

CHURCH

HIGHWAY 28

Contents

PROLOGUE

A wind ripped through the town, swirling clouds of dust nearly as high as the lonely café. A bright red neon sign burned through the blustery night adding a man-made buzz to Nature's howl. Inside the café, Tara slaved to clean and organize in the wake of the last wave of hungry truckers. Tall, lean and not nearly as athletic as she looked, Tara bumped a table. A sugar glass knocked onto its side and rolled, making that sound, the one equal to $1.95 off her paycheque.

But when the roll ended there was no crash. Tara glanced over her shoulder and saw a teenaged boy standing behind her. She gasped and jumped as though the soles of her shoes had suddenly turned to hot coals. The tub of dishes she carried dropped to the floor, everything within it smashing into pieces.

The teen stepped forward, holding out the sugar jar. He said, with a voice that rasped, "At least I was able to save one."

Tara was speechless. She stared at him. He was short, broad-shouldered and very well-muscled. His brow sat low over his eyes, his mouth wrinkled from what must have been a lifetime of frowns. He had high cheekbones and stubbled cheeks. Dark sunglasses hid his eyes, and when he removed them his bright emerald gaze was like casting a hot iron rod into cold water. She forced herself to laugh in hopes of hiding her nervousness.

"I am so sorry," she said as she kneeled to clean up the mess.

"I startled you. It is I who should apologize."

Tara shifted. As she carefully picked up the shards of glass she asked, "Can I get you anything?"

He was silent. All was silent. Even the pieces of plate that Tara moved from the floor to the tub made no noise against each other. She stared at a long narrow piece, grabbed it like a knife, and shivered as though the room temperature had dropped twenty degrees.

He spoke, "Is there a back door?"

Tara tried to stand but could not. She tried to raise her weapon but could not. She could only whisper, "Uh, yeah."

"Then leave everything behind and follow me. Or tonight you die."

Thoughts of the emergency buzzer flooded her mind. The fact that they'd placed it behind the cash register never seemed absurd until now.

She said, "You can take whatever you want. Please don't hurt me."

The stranger moved with a fluidity that appeared as if he'd materialized before her. Grabbing her shoulders he lifted her, stared into her eyes, eyes filled with tears, and said, "Please. I beg of you, follow me or tonight you will die."

Tara stood to her full height and shook off his grasp. Throwing the tub at him she ran for it, never looking back, not stopping to grab her purse or her jacket. She burst through the back door, leaving it helpless against the strong winds, hearing it bang against its frame. She ran into the pitch black night, into Cotter's field, engulfed in stalks of corn. Never before now did it seem so hard a task to avoid tall plants and furrowed mud. She tripped, fell against several corn stalks, and landed face first in the mud. When she lifted her head there was a tall, thin man clad in beggar's clothes before her. Tara screamed and jumped, slipping and landing hard on her back. It had been ten degrees that day and not much less this night yet her breath still formed tiny puffs of frozen air. She shivered, her heart beat fast and tears continued to flow. Muscles ached and seized. This time it was only a scarecrow, but whoever was out there made a noise crashing through the crops straight for her.

Stars and a full moon lighted the sky above. The wind howled, but for a brief moment when the bay of a wolf, carried by the cry of a man, echoed in the cornfield. Not as two cries but as one.

Tara closed her eyes and buried her face in her palms. Her body shook, her world collapsed. If the sanctity of a manmade environment, with all its electronic surveillance, could not protect her, then how safe was she surrounded by a farmer's crop? She had to keep moving until she found safety! She rose. But a hand from behind thrust her back to the ground. Tara screamed.

A man said, "I am prayer answered, I am salvation!" He walked in front of her and opened his arms wide. He stood tall and displayed a Mr. Universe physique. He wore a Vietnam vet's wardrobe and had weapons. A halberd strapped on his back, a crossbow on his belt. He looked as though he were a cross between Conan the Barbarian and Commando.

Tara didn't care. This man, whoever he might be, was her only escape from whatever was hunting her. She ran to him and wrapped her arms around his neck. As she sobbed into his chest she heard a clickety-click but did not realize what had happened until it was too late.

"What – what are you doing?"

As he handcuffed her to the scarecrow she struggled against him. He did not seem aware of her fight as he said, "Have you ever wished it in your power to act for the greater good?"

"What?"

"Have you ever felt powerless against evil and wished there was something you could do?"

"Yes, but…"

He cupped her chin in his palm and directed her teary gaze into his. "Your sacrifice will save hundreds."

Pulling free his survival knife he sliced her arm elbow to shoulder. Tara screamed. The man disappeared into the field. The wind calmed. Silence rose. The stars shone so bright it seemed they might set the world on fire. The moon glared like an ethereal Cyclops.

A wolf howled.

Tara stifled another scream. She yanked at the cuffs, then on the beam to which she was bound. Neither would give. Warm blood poured from the gash in her arm and formed a pool on the dry sod. It filled in cracks and ran towards the café. Tears fell from her chin and mixed with the crimson stream.

Heavy breathing nearby. Panting? Behind her. A man? Animal! Advancing? On her! Paws? Hands! Teeth! Tara closed her eyes as the beast wrapped its jaw around her neck. She did not look to see what it was that pushed two teeth, like tiny needles, through her neck and into her flesh.

Suddenly the creature slammed its entire body into her, knocking what wind she had left from her lungs. It was "Conan the Barbarian" who had drop kicked the beast with no regard for her safety. Tara struggled to get on the opposite side of the beam as Conan grappled with the … man? It looked human! It stood tall and lean, with short, blonde hair. It donned a long black coat but had mist for legs. Tara did not understand what was happening. She wondered what had happened to the man in the café.

That's when she saw it. A small metal key reflected in the mud by the moonlight. Conan the Barbarian must have dropped it! Lying as flat as she could, Tara stretched her long legs, just managing to pull the key through the sod. When it was close enough to grab, she did. She fit it into the handcuff's lock. The brace opened. Tara was free. She stood and ran like never before. Even when she tripped, even when her head spun from loss of blood, she continued to run. She crashed through the field. Scrambled out the other side onto the empty dirt road. And once there she stopped, breathless and panicked. Far off to the north, lights glowed from the small town. Tara stared at them, on her knees, sobbing and shivering. She could not rise above her knees, though the full extent of terror did not come to her at that moment.

But when it did, she understood, for the last few seconds of her life, what true horror was.

CHAPTER 1

"I hate this town," Kharl told his friends as he glared at the group of Native teens who had entered the burger joint.

"Want to leave? We could take the girls to Sunset Park," Simon said, stretching his arm around Betty. She snuggled close to her protector.

"No way. This is our booth, our joint, and our town. I ain't leaving just 'cause that dick is here."

Kharl's glare never left the bigger of the Native teens, nor did he back off from the glare returned to him. Alix, sitting beside him, rubbed the bottom of her nose with her left index finger out of nervous habit.

"What are you doing?" she asked.

"Nothing. Relax, there's only three of them."

"There's six, genius."

"But three are girls."

"That means they still outnumber you by one."

"So the odds are even." Then he said to the one whom he stared at: "Got a problem, Indian?"

The teen moved toward Kharl but a girl stopped him. "Don't, Derrik! It's what he wants."

Derrik stared at her with cold, blank eyes. "Maybe it's what I want." Then he said to Kharl: "You want me to kick your pink butt black and blue? Watch your mouth."

"Watch my mouth? Don't play this game if you ain't prepared to lose." Kharl stood and took off his jacket.

The windows rattled from a gust of wind.

At the same time Kim moved in front of Derrick, Alix grabbed Kharl's shoulder. Both girls whispered, "Let's go somewhere else."

"I'm not afraid of that loser!" Kharl stepped into the aisle.

Derrick moved his sister aside and glowered at Kharl. "What did you call me?"

Alix looked at Kim pleadingly, but the Native girl stared back for only a second. Her muscles turned rigid, her lips pursed, and her eyes grew as cold as the bitter air outside. Alix sat, suddenly aware of the aroma of burgers frying.

"What's your problem?" Betty asked Alix. When she did not respond, Betty added, "Do you want Kharl to ask you to the dance?"

Alix smiled and her eyes grew distant. "Sorry."

Kharl glanced at the booth and winked at Alix. Then he turned back to Derrick, grabbing him roughly by the shoulders. Derrick pushed back and yelled, "Come on! Let's go!"

"What the hell is going on out here?" Bob the proprietor yelled, rushing from the kitchen. His grease-stained apron barely fit over his belly, but his powerful voice and towering height kept most troublemakers in line.

Kim turned to him first, "All we wanted was a warm place to go ... they started it!"

Bob walked behind Derrick and grabbed him, throwing the Native youth hard toward the door. "I never want to see you in here again!"

"I didn't even start it! Why don't you throw them out too?"

Bob took a step toward him, but stopped when he saw a knife in the teen's hand. Derrick glared at Kharl.

"Tomorrow morning meet me in Dead Man's Alcove. We'll settle this once and for all!"

"I'll kick your ass! Hell of a way to start the first day of school," Kharl shouted as his adversary left.

Bob turned to him. "You okay?"

"Yeah. Punk doesn't scare me." Then he said to his friends, "Let's get out'a here."

"Where?" Simon asked.

"The park, or wherever. Just not here."

"Got juice?"

"Course."

Then they left.

CHAPTER 2

Alix stared at her locker. This would be the final ten months that it would be packed with her entire life – books, love notes, pens and assignments. All the essentials that seemed so important but soon would be nothing but trash.

Betty had more clothes and make-up than actual school stuff in hers. She was not exactly a bookworm, but still somehow a solid "B" student. How Betty managed good grades without studying or doing homework no longer seemed important with the end so near. Betty smiled, her slender and curvy body beaming with energy. Her long, dark hair was loose and straight. She wore purple lipstick, fake eyelashes and black nail polish.

"Can you believe it's almost over? We'll finally be out of this prison!" Betty said.

Alix smiled, sighed and said, "Out of the zoo and into the wild."

"Huh?"

"Nothing." Alix looked about herself, slowly turning in a circle. This place had been her entire life for six years. She recalled the first week of secondary school when she had somehow separated from the orientation group and got lost. And the time in grade nine when a boy first asked her out on a date. He may have been a geek but it sure felt special at the time. Then there was grade ten when Betty joined cheerleading and became popular. That year Alix was left behind in teenage obscurity. And now, here she was, at the end of high school. Her last chance to be one of the popular girls. She sighed.

"Oh my," Betty whispered. "You'll never guess who's coming."

"Who? Kharl?" Alix said, hope strong in her voice.

"See you later," Betty said with a mischievous smile. Then, walking away, she sang, "Don't do anything I *would* do."

Alix sighed and turned back to her task. Kharl walked up beside her, leaned against the locker by placing his palm flush against the metal frame. His letterman's jacket opened, his tight shirt hinting of a very muscular chest. *Oh my,* Alix thought.

"You just missed Betty." She hoped he wouldn't notice the tremble in her voice.

"I didn't come to see Betty. I came to see you."

Alix blushed and tossed her hair over her shoulders as she turned to look at him. "Really?"

"Yeah." His eyes shone bright blue and his toothy grin formed dimples in his cheeks. "You hear about Tara?"

Alix felt her heart sink. Tara was tall, raven-haired, athletic and exotic in a way that she could never be. It made sense that the star football hero would ask her out. Staring into her locker she said, "She was in my Lit class last year."

"She got attacked by a wolf just outside the Farcus Café last night."

Alix suddenly felt terrible for the jealousy that had

consumed her only moments earlier. Standing to face Kharl she asked, "Is she alright?"

"No. In the worst possible way." He looked serious. "I heard a rumor you ain't comin' to my party tonight and thought it might be about that."

Betty! Alix screamed silently. Her cheeks burned and her breath was hard to catch. "I, uh, just don't, you know, fit in."

He laughed, loudly. Then he met her eyes again and smiled. "What are you talkin' about, girl? If you don't fit in would I be here askin'," he dropped to his knees and several passing students took notice, "beggin', I am beggin you to come."

Alix couldn't wipe the smile from her face. Burying her face in her palms, she started to laugh. Then she met his beautiful eyes. "Okay, I'll come. Okay!"

"Revelry starts at ten!"

"I still can't believe you're having a party so early."

"Hey, if they're gonna have the first day of school on a Friday then we're gonna party hard!" He started to walk away but stopped to add, "You comin' to watch my fight in Dead Man's Alcove?" Kharl held out his hand to her.

"Uh, sure." Alix felt silly with such a big smile. Taking his hand she walked with him.

Derrick stormed into the alcove followed by six of his buddies and Kim clinging to his black leather jacket. Tears rolled from her eyes.

"Please! Don't fight!" she begged.

"Kim! Don't embarrass me!"

Kim whispered, "Then don't fight."

Derrick closed his eyes a moment and ground his teeth. When he met her eyes he spoke through snarling lips, "Do you want to be one of them, Kim? Is that what you think is going to happen? Go over there. Try and be their friend. You know what they'll tell you? You're just a stupid Indian."

"And what will fighting prove?"

Derrick glared at his enemy and snapped, "It'll prove I'm not a stupid Indian."

Kharl glared back and handed his jacket to Simon. "Look at this guy. He's lucky I didn't put him in his place long ago."

"Check out the silver studs on his jacket. Careful he doesn't use them as a weapon."

Derrick pushed his sister aside and said, glaring straight at Kharl, "Screw 'em."

Alix watched from within the gathering crowd as the two adversaries faced off. Betty, who was pulling incessantly on her arm like a two-year-old child, squealed, "You must be so proud of your boyfriend!"

"He's not my boyfriend." Alix smiled and blushed, turning to a window that had started rattling from the gusty breeze outside. She stared past its pane at the green field that never ended, as if it were an ocean with grass for waves. Betty glanced at it for a second, and then started pulling on Alix's arm again.

"Well, not yet," Betty said. Then she shrieked, "It's about to start!"

Alix turned her focus on the impending battle. She hoped Kharl wouldn't get a black eye from this with the school dance just next week. Not that he'd asked her. Would he ask her? She couldn't help smiling thinking that Kharl might actually ask her!

Kharl and Derrick locked eyes, each daring the other to back down. They circled one another as if they were beasts of prey warring over the same lair. Kharl first pushed Derrick, who shoved back at Kharl. Finally they grabbed one another, when suddenly a deep voice from beside them growled, "Excuse me."

The two adversaries looked at one another. Who would be brave enough to interrupt their fight? Even the teachers made a point of staying away whenever students settled disputes. They looked and saw a short, stocky youth clad in an open grey leather jacket, baggy black sweats, and a white muscle shirt. Hair, darker than any night, crowned his head like a lengthy headdress. Thick eyebrows met together above his narrow, emerald eyes, and when this outsider spoke, his voice came out in a raspy banter that nearly hid a hint of a Gaelic accent. A low, menacing growl trailed his breaths and, again, the stranger snarled, "Excuse me."

Kharl looked at Derrick to see if he might have an explanation of who this guy thought he was. Derrick didn't, so Kharl decided to take care of things himself. Glaring at the stranger as if to say: "Excuse me? Get lost! We're busy!" he grabbed Derrick and again prepared to fight.

But this stranger did not want to leave things alone. This time he reached between them with his bulky arm, saying directly to Kharl, "Excuse me!" and, with a little more forced clarity in his words, he said to Derrick, "For the last time!"

They tried to move his arm but as they did the slack in his jacket tightened with a steel-like texture. Kharl and Derrick formed an unspoken truce to square off against the stranger instead of each other, with Kharl moving in first to deal with this outsider. This jock wasn't afraid of their new foe's sculpted appearance, but when their eyes met in challenge Kharl received a glare so fierce that his skin turned pale. The students watched in awe as their prized football star ran from the alcove with no explanation.

Alix thought she should go after Kharl. Was this a good time to be there for him, or should she wait? As if answering her thoughts Betty said, "You can go to Kharl after this jerk gets his butt kicked."

The outsider still had another adversary with whom to contend. Derrick didn't hesitate to take Kharl's place, and, shoving his opponent in the chest, Derrick spit on the stranger's shoes. The outsider didn't budge, not even an inch.

"What the hell do you want in Dead Man's Alcove?" Derrick turned to ensure his gang waited to back him up before facing the stranger to add, "You want me to make you a permanent resident?"

Derrick wouldn't break his lock with the stranger's sunken gaze. They stood nose to nose, the stranger breathing hard in loud, raspy growls. Suddenly Derrick grabbed his temples and shook his head as if fighting off some unseen force. The crowd stepped back.

Then Derrick threw the first punch.

The alcove echoed with cheers as everyone watched the stranger reel from the blow. He threw his face back and licked his lips as if tasting blood, though no one could see any. When the stranger levelled his vision Derrick hauled off again, threw a second punch, but this time the stranger deftly caught the hurtling fist. Squeezing it tightly he brought Derrick to his knees, wincing with pain.

Alix wondered if Derrick's gang might step in, but they looked at a loss for what to do.

"We can choose our lockers?" he snarled in a deep, raspy voice.

"Screw off."

The stranger appeared as unconcerned with Derrick's dignity as he did of the gang who had begun gathering around him. Alix expected them to jump him, maybe shank him and leave him for dead, but they did nothing more than witness their leader's plummeting reputation.

"I asked," the stranger began cooly. Then, as he broke Derrick's fingers, he said, "We-can-choose-our-lockers?"

"Yes!" Derrick yelled in agony, unable to hide the tears pouring from his eyes. But the tears hadn't surprised his gang nearly as much as the tone in his voice, for borne in that tone resounded something no one had ever thought they'd hear from him – a hint of pleading.

The outsider released his captive, and, as the slack in his jacket grew taut from his tensed muscles, he shouted loudly so the whole student body would hear, "Then I choose this one!" And he glared, as if to tell anyone else who might think to challenge him to settle their claim then and there.

With that echoing through Fillmore High's hallowed halls, the sacred locker, the one belonging to the spirit doomed to haunt the students forever, again became occupied.

Quite unchallenged.

As the students dispersed from Dead Man's Alcove he paid no more attention to them. He examined his locker, giving the impression that he was a person content with being left alone. A demand for which they all gave respect.

Betty grabbed Alix's arm. "Let's go, girl. Your boyfriend really needs your support."

"He's not my boyfriend ... why don't you go without me?"

Betty placed her hand on her hip and smiled, tilting her head. "And just what are you going to do?"

Alix watched the new kid hang his jacket on a hook inside his locker. He carried a knapsack, and looking at it he sighed. Alix's heart swelled and she felt drawn to him, unsure as to why.

"I'm going to talk to him."

"Are you crazy?"

"Why don't you come with me?"

"If you go talk to him girl, you're on your own."

"Fine. Forget it then." Alix turned from the alcove and started to follow Betty out. But she stopped, her heart again yearning to know him. Alix rubbed the bottom of her nose and said, "I'm going to talk to him. If you don't want to fine, but I am."

"It's not cool, baby. Don't ruin all my hard work getting you 'in'." Betty waited a few seconds before rolling her eyes and leaving.

Alix stood alone with the stranger in Dead Man's Alcove, and taking a deep breath for courage she walked toward him. She wondered if his locker door blinded him from her approach, so she waited for him to notice her. When he didn't, Alix said, "Hi. My name's Alexandria, but my friends call me Alix. Sorry 'bout Derrick and Kharl."

The new student closed his locker and met her golden-hazel eyes. She stopped speaking. His eyes turned misty, and his brow relaxed. He wrapped his arms around his chest and sighed, parting his lips slightly as if he wanted to speak but didn't know what to say. Alix felt a wave of emotion wash over her like none other she had experienced. It was as though she were in one of those movies where the camera suddenly starts spinning around the actors, the motion creating a dizzying feeling that takes the audience outside of the moment and into a place on the edge of time and space. She stepped back, kept her eyes locked with his and slowly reached out to caress his stubbled cheek as one might do to help ease a friend's melancholy.

But before her hand reached his cheek, he gently redirected it. His touch stopped the spinning and brought her back to this moment. The one where she was standing before a potentially violent teen. They were now alone in the alcove, a place in the school that was completely soundproof. As the stranger opened his locker door to place his book bag inside, she said nothing further.

Just before she could turn and leave he secured his locker with a combination lock and walked out from the alcove.

"What a freak!" she thought as chills cascaded through her spine like little laughs mocking her for thinking to welcome him.

"Perhaps you should have just let him be," a voice said within her subconscious.

"Who's that?" Alix replied aloud, looking all around

herself in the empty alcove.

"Your conscience," the voice told her. *"If you want to help him, show him to his class. Look how lost he is."*

This wasn't the usual way her conscience spoke to her. Normally it came through emotions, an intuition that led her to do the "right" thing. She had, for the most part, stopped listening to that part of her, mostly due to the fact that it was this very conscience that had kept her from being popular. But here it was, her conscience, telling her what to do in a voice that seemed foreign to her.

"Not important," Alix decided as she rushed to catch up with the stranger. Forcing her full red lips into a smile, she asked him, "So, where are you off to?"

He stopped his crawl, examined his timetable, and turned to her. He avoided making eye contact. Alix wondered if his darkness existed only in her mind ... that perhaps what had happened earlier was just bad circumstance. But when next he spoke his voice again came in such a low, raspy tone that she questioned whether she should have just let him be.

"History. Mister Pausron's class," he said.

"That's my class, too." She bit her lip. "I can show you where it is."

As Alix walked beside the stranger, she turned so she could look at him. Whenever his eyes met hers he diverted them as if to hide something. She wondered what a complete stranger could possibly have to hide.

"We're here," she said when they came to a door marked 1H-6. She smiled and made a motion with her hand that he should enter first.

The new kid paused, and there was a sparkle in his

sunken emerald eyes that warmed his aura. But again the harsh, pensive look returned as the stranger indicated that she should enter first. Alix did not argue. As she walked down the aisle a sensation began in the back of her mind as if someone had set a fire. Slowly, as it engulfed her entire spirit, the sensation made the journey feel as if a magical whirlwind had trapped her in another era of time. She closed her eyes to shake this unnatural feeling from her soul but was unable to do so.

Claiming her usual seat, Alix noted that the only empty places were Betty's beside her and one in the far back. The stranger glanced at the one beside her, and she wondered which he might take. He smiled, but continued his way toward the back. Alix's tense muscles melted as the aura about her lost its eerie sensation.

"Did you talk to him?" Betty inquired, taking her usual seat while trying to capture Alix's averting gaze.

"Not really. He only let me show him to the class."

Betty shook her head and rolled her eyes. "He looks evil. Kharl was pretty mad you didn't go to him."

"What's the big deal that I wanted to welcome a new student?"

"I don't know what your problem is, girl. What's with the charity case?" she glanced back to where the stranger had sat next to Simon. "Great. He's sitting next to my boyfriend. Hope he doesn't start anything."

"Who? The new guy, or Simon?"

"What was that?"

Alix sighed. "Nothing."

"I don't understand what you're thinking, girl."

"Good-morning, class," said a tall, thin man clad in grey cords and a blue sweater as he strolled into the room.

"Morning, Mister Pausron," the class responded in unison, their conversation cut short by his sharp smile.

Mister Pausron stopped in front of his desk, sat on its top as he always did, and smiled.

"I hope you all had as enjoyable a holiday as I."

Reaching behind him for the class roster, he noticed a new face in the room. Scanning the list until he came across an unfamiliar name penciled in by the principal he closed his eyes and committed the name and face to memory. "I see a new person in here. Rellik Faolchú. Welcome. I hope you enjoy our sleepy little town, and I hope your parents don't change their minds about staying after last night's unusual wolf attack."

"Wolf attack?"

Charles looked for who had spoken and found Simon with a smile plastered on his face. "Please, Simon…."

"I heard it was a person … a cannibal! … that just made it look like a wolf did it." Simon's tapping foot echoed in the silence.

Charles said, "Perhaps a werewolf? Did you learn nothing from the tragedy of '89? Orphans were killed, a boy disappeared and the Tannis family was murdered. Rumors don't solve anything." Charles wanted to continue the discussion, but, glancing at the clock, he knew if he did there wouldn't be enough time left for the lesson he had planned. Still, he also saw from the look on many of his students' faces that the previous night's tragedy troubled them. Worse, many believed Simon's "werewolf" concoction. He really had meant to speak with Simon's father about his son's tendency to disrupt class, but for now he had a class full of scared teens and a new student to introduce.

"Class, before we continue on this subject, and we can continue should any of you have concerns, we have a new student to welcome. Rellik, why don't you take center stage and introduce yourself. Tell us where you come from and, perhaps, something we should know about you. Stand, please."

Rellik's square jaw drew tense and he didn't rise. He glared hard, his long, cold stare captivating his audience just as a cobra might captivate its prey moments before lashing out with its venomous bite.

"My name is Rellik Faolchú. There is nothing more about me that any of you needs to know."

Rellik fixed his glare on Mister Pausron and set the stage for a challenge.

"So be it, Rellik. That is your right."

Mister Pausron had looked forward to this first school day all summer. But had he known how unusually long and intensely uncomfortable it was going to be, he may not have wanted it to come at all.

Alix skipped her afternoon Math period to sit alone in the library. She couldn't help but obsess over the new kid. He seemed so tense, so uncomfortable, so ready to explode. Yet she felt a need to understand where he came from and who he could be.

There was only one computer in the entire school dedicated for student use. It was a clunky museum piece with an incredibly slow dial-up modem. Minitaw was so far in the dark ages that it was beyond sad. Alix couldn't wait to move to the city for university.

"Okay, Rellik Faolchú, let's see who you are."

Alix typed his name (guessing on the spelling of his surname) and made sure to put them in quotes like Fred, her own personal techie, had taught her. Google took forever to bring up a response, which added to the frustration that it had come up with nothing. She tried just "Rellik" but even after the longest twenty seconds of her life it came up dry. Should she try just his surname? Alix sighed and was ready to give up. But as the wind outside rattled the pane behind her, Alix absently tried, "FAHLCHOO". It came up with zero except... "Did you mean FAOLCHU?" Clicking on the link she waited almost sixty seconds for sixty thousand hits.

"Useless," she whispered as she clicked on the third link down that brought her to an Irish mythology site. On the cover page she read:

"Rancour, son of Faolchú, was born c.988. After his clan of shape shifters was slaughtered by the Alsandair, a nomadic tribe, he was kidnapped and raised with no knowledge of his heritage.

"The Alsandair were famous for their war-like ways, and they believed that Rancour would breed his supernatural abilities into their race..."

And blah, blah, blah, so it read. *What kind of geek would write a website like this?* Alix wondered. She looked about herself to make sure that no one was around, and when she was satisfied that no one was close enough to peer over her

CHAPTER 2

shoulder she brought up her blog. Clicking on the icon for "new entry" she began to type:

"Weird day. Kharl still hasn't asked me out, but Betty keeps hinting that he will soon. I think he's waiting for the dance. I'm hoping he's going to ask me to it."

Suddenly, that strange sensation came over her again, the same one that had encircled her outside of Mr. Pausron's class when she was standing with Rellik. She started to type:

"My parents have both died from a terrible illness. The townsfolk took them away today, to burn their bodies so they don't spread the disease. I fear that it may be too late. My brother has started a terrible cough and twice now he has woken with blood on his lips."

The school clock buzzed as the large hand struck twelve in the afternoon, but in Alix's world the sound went unnoticed. She continued to write, until someone threw a book on the table.

"Hi, Alix." It was Fred. "Working through lunch? Want me to leave you alone?"

"No, don't be silly. I'll work on this later." She scrambled to get it off the screen.

"You sure?" He sat in a chair across the table from her. "Hey, that's cool. Writing assignment for English class?"

"Uh, no. I wasn't working on school stuff." Alix looked at him, smiling in hopes he'd just forget about it. And he would, just like always.

That's why Fred was so comfortable to be around: his predictability. He was wearing the same outfit that he had worn all last year. She wondered if his closet was all just

25

one outfit, like that Einstein guy was supposed to have. She thought it funny that he wore his old clothes even though it was the first day of a new school year. But Fred wasn't at fault for that, nor was he at fault for his matching grey slacks and black shoes that looked like two little mirrors. His parents controlled whatever he wore, all the way from his tie clip to the haircut that screamed future banker.

His apparel was a major reason why she had never spoken to him before this past summer. Fred had his own unique charm that you had to get used to, just like the Icy Shakes' burgers. But now that they were friends, Alix never let his freak status bother her.

"So why are you here, anyway? Don't you ever eat?" she asked.

"I can both study and eat. You, uh, hear about the fight?"

"Yeah. I take it you heard."

"Hard not to. I heard the new guy beat up both Derrick and Kharl."

"Why, Fred! Is that pleasure in your voice?"

He blushed. "You know I abhor violence ... but those two sure need an ego check."

"Well, I hate to burst your bubble, but only Derrick got his ego checked."

Fred perked an eyebrow.

"Okay, so technically Kharl ran away, but he didn't lose."

"Is that how he's rationalized it?"

Alix laughed. "Yeah. Y'know, you're going to mess things up for me with this whole 'reality' thing."

"I heard you talked to the new kid."

"I'm not making that mistake twice!"

"Why? What happened?"

"It's weird. You look in his eyes and it's like looking into another world."

"Do we know anything about him?"

"Nope. Maybe you can Google him for me later."

Fred smiled. "Googling for answers, young Jedi? So your training is complete." Then, more seriously, he asked, "What's this fascination about?"

The school bell rang, indicating the end of lunch. Fred said, as Alix gathered her things, "Saved by the bell."

"We'll talk later," Alix said.

"Anytime. You, uh, doing anything tonight?"

"No," she lied. "But if I change my mind I'll call you. See ya."

Alix hurried down the hall to her English Lit class. But at the door she realized she'd forgotten her Hamlet text.

"Damn," she whispered, spinning to go back to her locker.

Kim was standing in the hallway not five feet from Alix. Kim's eyes were as piercing as her brother's knife. Alix thought to just ignore her and walk past, but Kim moved purposefully to block her way. Now they were mere inches apart. Alix stepped to the left, Kim followed in suit. Alix tried the right, Kim still blocked her.

"Uhh..." Alix looked around but everyone had gone to class. They were alone.

"Why are you afraid of me?" Kim asked with obvious disdain.

"I'm not," Alix laughed with a trembling voice.

"So you are just another Barbie wannabe that thinks all us Indians are gang members."

Alix didn't know how to get out of this. She could scream and get the teachers out here, but she wasn't sure she still had a voice.

"I was so wrong about you." Kim shook her head and turned to walk away.

"Wait." Alix found her courage buried beneath her curiosity. "Wrong about what?"

"Last night at Icy Shakes, you were the only one who didn't seem to want a fight to happen."

"I didn't want a fight to happen."

"Well, I just thought you and I could stop this stupid pissing contest between your boyfriend and my brother. But forget it."

Alix watched as Kim walked away. She did want to stop the fight between Kharl and Derrick, but she was already in enough trouble with Kharl. Thankfully she was still invited to his party, and hopefully she hadn't erased all her chances of getting asked to the dance! Alix decided to forget this incident with Kim. That was the only option.

CHAPTER 3

That evening a chill wind swept over the sleepy town, bringing a grim reminder that winter would soon besiege them. Alix spent the evening at home, hiding on the sidelines, waiting for Betty to call about Kharl's party. She didn't spend much time at home anymore, at least not since Lymphatic-Leukemia had stolen her mother two years ago. That was the last time she'd seen strength in her father and in her family.

Her mother's passing had forced Alix to grow up quickly, for during the past two years not only had she seen to her own care but to Sam's as well. Alix glanced at where she usually left the phone and saw that it wasn't there. She wondered if she'd left the ringer on and considered going downstairs to get it. But the thought of seeing her drunk father stumble around the house changed her mind.

If it had been warm, she would have rested in the gazebo that stood at the back of their garden, and had it been daytime she would have tended the flowers. But on this cold evening she desired the warmth of her room. With book in hand she walked to her wicker chair and sank deeply into the soft cushions, with only the bright overhead lamp that hung above her by golden chains for company, its fellowship casting a mirror against her large bedroom window. Sometimes when Alix glanced at her reflection she had to look twice, for every now and then she didn't recognize the pensive image who stared back.

Her room faced the field behind her home where she could look on to the end of the Earth. A narrow stairwell that rose into the loft above their garage passed just below the sill, where her mother had once painted in hopes of becoming world-famous. As a young girl Alix has visited that loft often to watch her work, but since her death she could not bring herself to visit it again. As Alix stared at the girl in the mirrored window she turned a page in the book that rested in her curled lap, recalling that she had homework to do.

The stairwell just outside her door creaked and footsteps clip-clopped against the silence, interrupting her thoughts. Alix knew it was her father, probably wanting her to cook his dinner. She glanced at the digital alarm clock beside her bed and saw that it read 6:13 pm. She sighed, hoping that this time he'd just make his own dinner.

Her father opened the door beside her wicker chair, but Alix refused to face him. She called him "Sam" for spite rather than "dad." Alix now turned to face her father, taken aback by what she saw.

He was not at all what she had grown accustomed to expect. He was clean-shaven, showered and smelled of Old Spice. His thinning blond hair was cut and styled neatly to one side, and he wore over his hefty six-foot build a grey suit with a tie and a rose in the left pocket. The most striking thing, and the most pleasing, was that her father hadn't been drinking! For the first time in three years he bore a look of optimism rather than defeat.

"Alexandria," Sam said, the words creating a sound that

was not as hopeful as his demeanour, "I'm going to interview people. I'm hiring help ... for the store, I mean. I'm ... I'm reopening." Sam paused as if to let her open up to him, but Alix didn't know what she should say. His shoulders slumped and his eyes glistened from tears held at bay. "If the phone rings, would you answer it?"

Her father broke eye contact with her, but Alix still stared at him in shock. There was so much she wanted to say, but the rush of emotions stunned her. A part of her wanted to bound from the wicker chair and grab him in a hug, to break into a cry with such reverence that her tears would shed his past years of drunkeness. But another part remembered the two years he had forced her to go at life alone, and that part wished to damn him. She stared at her father and managed to say only, "Okay."

Sam smiled his first genuine, sober grin in years and gently closed the door behind him. He knew the news had overwhelmed her. Hell, even he was having difficulty accepting the situation. This hadn't been an easy decision to come to, and clearing his throat in hopes it might calm his nerves, he wondered if he'd see his decision through to its end. He could, after all, live a few more years off his wife's insurance money, but ... a long time ago he had made a promise to her. A promise he had neglected these last two years.

Sam fixed his tie and jacket as he descended the creaky stairwell, thinking how good it felt to know he might be part of his daughter's life again. Time had passed so quickly that when he looked at her she seemed almost like a stranger. A small chuckle escaped his throat when he realized that he was even a stranger to himself. He needed to change so many things that there seemed too many first steps to take.

Sam decided to wait until later to tell her he had joined Alcoholics Anonymous and inform her about Alateen. He accepted that fact that his drinking had grown way beyond a temporary crutch and into a deadly obsession. Two full years had passed since he was last sober, and recalling the years previous to his wife's passing, there hadn't been many days of sobriety then either. He had wallowed in self-pity for too long and needed to get on with life, but for it to feel worth living he needed his daughter to be a part of it.

As he walked into his dark den, Sam rubbed the brass door handle and made a special note to shut the door. Its icy touch soothed him, and as he ran another finger down the door's wood grain, he wondered if he'd ever be able to accept his wife's passing without his crutch. If only he could be as strong as Alexandria maybe he wouldn't be so alone ... perhaps he could find another?

Sam turned on the overhead lamp, looked at his den, and smelled the musk from the time he had spilled his aftershave. The carpet still stank, but he had kept it because he and his wife had picked it together. He once used the room to prepare for hunting trips. Along one wall was a large bookcase for his hunting guides and directly across from it was a desk used to reload shells.

But every time he entered this place of solace none of these things caught his eye. To him the dominant item was his wife's portrait that hung over the mantel, and, resting below it, placed before his hunting rifle, was the urn holding her ashes. Sam stared at the urn, and as a familiar pain welled in his chest he knew that he would never be able to take that one final step and remarry. If he could not live out the rest of his days with Trina, then he would spend them alone. He would never replace her.

He walked to his sitting chair, slumped his shoulders and sighed. His grasp on hope weakened, and staring at the portrait he collapsed into his leather recliner. Sam wondered if he'd get through this night, let alone the rest of his life, without a drink.

He didn't even realize that he had grasped the bottle of whiskey that he kept stashed beside the chair.

The evening quickly matured into night and, though Sam had advertised in the local paper as well as the local employment agency, no one had come about the job. Alix rested upstairs in her room with the lights off and her Pooh Bear as a cuddly in her cozy wicker chair. She knew by now that Sam would have lost heart, and staring out her large glass window at the constellations so far away, she glimpsed a star shooting across the heavens. She wished upon it that there might be something she could do to help Sam, fearing greatly that she might lose him again. A single tear tickled as it made the lone journey down her cheek. She dared not touch it. She allowed it this sojourn, and when it reached her chin and clung as if for life, she prayed that Sam, like the tear, would cling to his life.

Her alarm clock read 9:22 pm. The evening had grown too late for anyone to come about the job, and that surprised her. She knew many people, mostly fellow students, who needed the work, and wondered why no one had come.

Then she remembered: Sam's reputation as a drunk. It saddened her that, though there were many in the small town who needed any kind of employment, no one wished to work with that "Conway loser."

Alix caught the clinging tear from her chin and held it gently in her palm. She closed her fingers over it; its cool touch on her warm skin was not unlike her sorrow for Sam. He must be aware that the town thought of him as nothing more than a drunk, and worse yet, so did she.

A loud, shrill ring ended the silence. Alix leaped from her wicker chair and flew down the staircase. She wished she'd come down earlier to bring the phone to her room, as the noise may have interrupted Sam. Before answering it, she peered down the unlit hall at the den and saw that the light emanating from the bottom of the door didn't flicker. She assumed the phone hadn't disturbed Sam, and by the beginning of the third ring, Alix turned on the receiver.

"Hello?" she sang, grabbing a folding chair and waiting for the person at the other end of the line to speak. Alix opened the chair to face south toward the front door with her back to the den and again said, "Hello?" this time a little louder. After she'd heard Betty's voice, she relaxed into the plastic folding chair.

"Hi, Betty! Guess what? Sam's reopening the store! Isn't that great?"

"Whatever. Are you going to Kharl's party or what? Last chance, baby!"

"Uhm, I was, but now I don't know."

"You will if you want him to ask you to Friday's school dance," Betty warned her.

Alix leaned against the cold wooden door, wishing the conversation could have been about Sam. But she did want popularity, and no matter how much she hated to admit it Betty knew the inner workings of boys more than she did.

"Can we go later?"

"Duh! Of course we'll go later. Meet me at my house and we'll fix you up. Baby, Kharl won't be able to resist!" Betty burst into a loud fit of giggles.

Even Alix giggled as she asked, "Do you really think he'll ask me?"

A loud knock returned Alix to the moment.

"Betty, I'll be there in half an hour!"

Alix sprang from her place against the door, hanging up without waiting for a response. As the loud knock resounded again, Alix faced the entryway, frozen like a statue, relieved that, at long last, someone had come for the job! She knew that above anything else this would lift Sam's spirits!

Sam could not move. The knock on the door made him wonder if someone in the town still believed in him. He pressed the bottle's mouth firmly against his lips, and breathing the heavy smell from the baiting liquid, he closed his eyes tight. Sam wondered if he still believed in himself.

Some unseen demon had magically petrified his legs and bound his neck. A whisper, one that lived deep in a part of his soul that he had hoped to end, reminded him how much easier this interview would be if only he'd take one drink. Just one ... the bottle was so close by, the liquid so easily accessible. A third and fourth hand closed around his own, and they forced him to grip the bottle tighter.

"*This is no longer your choice,*" the demon told him. "*One won't hurt. You will stop at one.*"

Suddenly, he heard the door to his den creak open and his daughter's light footsteps enter the room. Red-faced he turned to her ... noticing for the first time how much she resembled her mother, especially in her eyes. It was in that solemn gaze that he found his command to force the demon to lose his grip and vanquish.

"I'll be back!" the demon said as it left, and Sam knew it would make good on that promise.

Sam rose from his leather recliner just as his daughter opened her mouth to voice her obvious hurt. He gently capped the bottle as if he were afraid it might shatter and left it to rest on the recliner's arm. Wrapping his arms around his chest he slid his hands inside his jacket to hide the shaking that now besieged his entire body.

"Should I get the door?" she asked, holding her tears at bay.

"No," Sam answered in a deep throaty whisper, unable to meet her gaze. "I'll get the door. You dispose of this." He indicated to the bottle with a nudge of his head. "As well, clean out the cupboards ... including the hidden compartment under the kitchen sink."

The knock again resounded from the front door and they both knew they had to put this moment into the past. They followed one another from the den and parted, Alix south toward the kitchen and Sam north toward the front door. Alix paused to see who had come.

It was that new kid, Rellik. Or, at least that's who she thought it was. A shadow cast from the darkness outside made him appear more like an apparition than a person. He stood away from the doorway as if he didn't want the light from the house to touch him. His eyes, cringed against the light, glowed. Alix met them, but only for a moment, for he slapped on a pair of dark sunglasses as if to hide what his soul might betray. In that moment fear held her fast as though paralysis had overtaken her.

She wanted to flee, but her fright began taking shape in her mind. It became images, ones taken from the story she'd written earlier that day in her blog. Alix thought to speak to him, but when she tried her voice failed.

Rellik wrapped his arms tightly around his chest and sighed, his breath spitting in a low, raspy growl, "I'm here for the job." But whether the voice had come from him or from some deep recess in her mind, she did not know.

She wanted to answer for Sam, who just stood at the door, but as her hands trembled it was all she could do to hold onto the bottle. Alix felt like a prisoner to the outsider's strange power, and though she finally did break free enough to escape into the kitchen, the captor never did fully leave her heart.

When she heard the door to the den close, Alix crept back to eavesdrop. She wondered what Rellik wanted with this job, as customer service didn't really seem like his thing. She listened to them speak.

Sam said, "What's your name?"

"Rellik. Rellik Faolchú."

"What education do you have?" Sam's voice sounded monosyllabic. Alix wished she could see what was happening.

"I've enrolled at Fillmore High to complete my senior year."

"What about family? Where do they live?" This time,

as he asked the two questions, she wondered to herself, her father sounded more in control of his words. Alix waited impatiently for the answers, but there was a lull in the conversation before the outsider said:

"I have no family. As for my living arrangements, I thought you could let me stay in the loft above your garage instead of giving me full pay."

"I would need references…."

"I have no references."

"I'm sorry, Rellik. Without references I don't think…" Sam paused, and Alix knew something very odd was going on inside that den but what it was she just couldn't figure. "You're hired," her father said, his words robotic. Like someone who was hypnotized.

"And the loft?" Rellik asked with obvious confidence, as if he had pre-written the conversation and had only asked it to please himself.

"Of course." Sam's tone gave away what it was in his voice that seemed so familiar. It was the sound of control. An absolute, unyielding control. She wondered what kind of power Rellik possessed to grant him such dominion over another human being. She was reminded of the supernatural voice that had impersonated her conscience, and of how it had convinced her to show Rellik to their class. Then she remembered Kharl squaring off against Rellik. Kharl just started shaking his head from side to side, as if he were fighting something within his mind. Had he, too, heard the commanding voice?

Alix heard them shuffle and took it as an indication that the interview had ended. She rushed from her place by the door and hurried toward the kitchen, but when Rellik exited she turned to him. The door to the den remained open, yet only he had left, and when he turned to face her, they found themselves caught in the same position as when he had first entered the home. His gaze from beneath his shades penetrated her defences, and Alix shrank from him. He turned away, slumped his shoulders and sighed.

Without uttering a single word he left.

Sam still had not emerged from the room, and Alix ran to shut the front door. After throwing the bolt, a bolt they had never used, she turned her back on the secured door to face the den. She wondered if something had happened that she hadn't heard. Walking toward the quiet room she contemplated whether to enter, but she didn't want her father to think she didn't believe in him.

Just as she reached the doorway Sam suddenly bustled out into the hallway.

Alix knew he hadn't noticed her so she moved aside. He headed straight for the coat rack and when he grabbed his trench coat she thought, *Where is he going?*

He turned and glanced into her eyes, conveying an apology by his very stature.

"I never said this would be a miracle," Sam whispered just before he left.

Alix ran to her room, tears filling her eyes.

If Sam had witnessed that, he would have remarked at just how much his daughter had turned out like her mother.

CHAPTER 4

"It is better to die alone than to die surrounded by those who never truly cared. The one may be a tragedy, but the other is a lie.

"Yet to die in the arms of the one you love, to grow old and watch your love do the same, that is the greatest gift of all. For it is not death we fear so much as the circumstance in which it shall come."

                                                        –Wulfsign

B eer. Loud music. Dark rooms. Lots of obnoxious people. This was the part of high school life that Lara was going to miss. With beer in hand she wove her way through the crowded room. Remind the jocks of what they'll miss, let the geeks feel what they'll never have. Popularity. Power. Control.

The room spun just enough to make everyone sound interesting, and the bass on the dance music gave the room that special vibe that totally turned her on. Moving through the crowd she found her way to the couch and sat beside Gord. Lara handed him a beer.

Gord took a swig and leaned in to kiss her. Lara saw they had an audience, mostly the geeks. Lara leaned in to kiss him back and noticed his eyes were rolling into the back of his head.

"How much beer have you had, baby?"

He kept making out, even though his lips were nowhere near her. "I'll be fine, I'll be fine."

Lara pushed him off and fixed her blouse. Her heart beat fast and she definitely wasn't ready to call this a night. One guy, tall, wiry and kind'a Bill Gates-looking, stood alone in a corner. *Never had a geek before,* Lara thought and walked to him. He pretended not to notice as she stared into his pale face. She took another step closer, then another. He had his hand clenched around the neck of a beer bottle, and as she pressed herself against his chest she took his hand and brought the bottle to her lips.

"Are you into sharing?"

He didn't respond. He finally looked at her, and his mouth was slightly open, but barely a breath came out. As Lara slowly wrapped her lips tightly around his beer bottle she tipped some into her mouth. Letting his hand free she said, "C'mon. Let's take a walk."

"S-s-s-sure," he stuttered, wide-eyed.

"What's your name?" she asked.

"Lenny."

You were doomed from birth!

Lara took his trembling hand and led him across the crowded floor, out the back door, and into the backyard. They walked until they were well into the field and the house was no more than a spot of light in the distance.

"Massage my shoulders," Lara demanded and sat in the grass.

Lenny came up from behind her and nervously put his hands on her. He started to squeeze, but stopped when Lara cringed.

"Ow! Come on, Lenny! I'm a real girl, not someone you've met in a video game! Do it right."

He started poking with his fingers, but stopped again when Lara twisted away from him. "I can't believe what a loser you are!"

"I-I-I-I'm s-s-sorry!" Lenny stuttered before he ran back towards the house. Lara laughed at him, her voice echoing against the starlit sky.

Footsteps approached from behind, each one crunching the long dry grass. Lara asked, "Is this a real man?"

"Follow me, or tonight you will die." It wasn't a familiar voice that had spoken. It was deep, raspy and scary as hell. Lara couldn't move. Footsteps rushed around her until a man, her height with long dark hair and the most amazing emerald eyes, stood before her. He grabbed her shoulders and asked, "Do you want to live?"

"Yes," she said as tears ran down her cheeks.

"Then follow me, or you will die!"

She thrust herself forward and pulled free from his grasp. Lara ran and did not look back, but heard the sound of metal being pulled from leather. She ran toward the tiny spec of light, fast as she could, crying and wailing. A wolf howled, metal clanged against metal, and a scream echoed.

Lara's shins hit something hard and she flew forward. Her face smashed into the grass and mud was in her mouth. She must have landed on her nose as blood ran down her chin. Placing her palms against the ground she pushed herself up and slowly turned to see what had tripped her. Lenny, hog-tied with a gag in his mouth, struggled for freedom. His eyes begged her for help as did his muffled screams. Whoever had caught him had sliced open his arm from the shoulder to the elbow and it bled fast. Whoever had caught him was still out there! Not so far off in the field the clang of metal echoed across the prairies.

Lara screamed, turned to run, but her cries of terror were quickly silenced.

For as the Northern Lights flashed streaks of green, blue

and pink across the sky, she looked up to meet the face of death.

Alix was dressed in a tight black mini with a red sweater. Her hair was crimped and loose over her shoulders and she wore red lipstick. It was not exactly her usual attire, but Betty had insisted and she seemed to know what boys wanted. As she strolled through the crowded room, even over the loud dance beat, she heard whispered comments of disdain from girls and appreciation from boys. She stopped when she reached a comfortable spot against the wall.

Betty stood beside her and said, "See? Told you you looked hot!"

Alix crinkled her nose and smiled. "I do, don't I?"

Betty laughed and pointed at the couch. "Check it out! Gord's totally faced AND he's lost his pants!"

Both Betty and Alix laughed. Betty said, "I'm going to get a beer, you want?"

Alix got that look. Her eyes narrowed and she nibbled the inside of her bottom lip. Betty prodded, "One beer won't hurt. You are almost eighteen!"

"Okay!" she squealed. Betty looked around and found the keg. Three jocks were manning and when they saw Betty approach they poured her a beer.

Betty sang, "Thanks, boys. Got one for my friend?"

They looked at each other. Then one said, "Keg's dry. And that one's special for you."

Betty winked at him then handed it to Alix who asked, "What about you?"

"Kharl must have more in the kitchen. Be right back, baby."

Alix looked at the people around her as she sipped her foul tasting beer. They seemed surreal through the smoke-laden air, each one pounding back drink after drink. Everyone was here, the jocks, the drama club, the geeks and … her. Alone, by the wall. Where was Betty and what was taking her so long? Alix started to walk through the crowd, pushing through the drunken revellers, trying to ignore each time someone grabbed her butt. So this was what she'd been missing by not being popular.

Eventually she made it to the kitchen, but when she entered the whole world stopped. There was Betty, wrapped in an embrace with Kharl. Wrapped in an embrace with Kharl! Tears lay on the edge of Alix's eyes. Dropping her beer, she ran from the room and the house. She ran out the back door, into the darkness.

She ran until she stumbled over something. It was wet, sticky and smelled horrible. The scent overwhelmed her and falling to her knees she emptied her stomach. Alix looked down and saw blood. And as her vision focused to the darkness she saw the remains of what had to be a corpse.

A voice from behind her spoke: "You need not fear, your prayers have been answered."

Alix couldn't move a muscle. She tried to scream but had no voice. She shivered and again felt nauseous. The man walked to stand before her, uncaring of what he stepped into. He was tall, wide and unbelievably muscular. A halberd was strapped to his back. A handgun was holstered to his belt. A machete was sheathed against his chest. He had a short, spiky boxcut. His square jaw was bearded with heavy, thick, black hair. He reached out and caressed her cheek as tears started down them.

"Do you want to save hundreds?" he asked.

"Please don't hurt me," was all she could muster.

Then another voice, Rellik's, from behind said, "Run to me, Alix, or you will die."

And she did. Alix ran toward Rellik who stood against the darkness. The man chased after her, his heavy strides loud against the sod. Rellik reached into his coat and drew a long sword. Its blade was crimson, with black lettering and a hilt shaped into the head of a wolf. As Alix drew near, Rellik grabbed her hand.

When they touched, there was a charge that passed from him to her. The ground itself began to harden and solidify, the air about her froze like black ice. The man who clearly had meant to kill her had disappeared and so had Rellik.

Alix closed her eyes and screamed in silence. When she opened her eyes again she was in her room, tucked in her bed, gripping her grandmother's comforter to her neck for security. She held her eyes shut to ward off the darkness, unable to stop her body from shaking as beads of perspiration mixed with the tears that streamed down her puffy cheeks. Never had a dream been so vivid, nor so real. She mustered the courage to open her eyes a crack, half-expecting to still be in that field with the giant and Rellik. The wall's shadowed floral-patterns relaxed her. Her room was a sanctuary and she took special comfort in her giant Pooh Bear that sat in the wicker chair gently showered in moonlight.

Alix released her grasp from the comforter and rolled onto her side, feeling around for her Kleenex box. Grasping one she pulled it to her face, wiping away the tears.

Her clock read 4:00 am. When had she come home? What had happened with the crazy sword wielding freak? What about Rellik? Alix rubbed her swollen eyes with clenched fists and wondered what had happened. Had someone spiked her drink and she'd just had some psychotic episode? Or was there a murderous stranger? And what of Rellik and the strange charge from him to her? Then she recalled the boy who had handed Betty the beer and what he had said, *"This one's special for you."* Bastard! The only thing she knew for certain was that she wouldn't fall back asleep tonight. Climbing out from her warm bed she dragged her blanket to the wicker chair, nestled onto her Pooh Bear's lap, and relaxed as its arms embraced her. As she leaned her head against its chest, she stared out her window at the foreboding red moon.

CHAPTER 5

Rellik sat upon a wooden crate inside his loft, staring at a painting on an easel. Dawn broke through a window, caressing the painting's half-finished tender face. Doe eyes, a Mona Lisa smile, and long blonde hair came together to create more soul than any painting he had seen.

Rellik placed four crates together and cast a tarp over them for a bed. He had no pillow, nor any blankets. He had left his belongings, except for a palm-sized intricately carved wooden box, with his car hidden in the woods.

Rellik lay on his makeshift bed, wondering where he would ever find the strength to complete his task.

Wondering if the identity he had once clung to had slipped away....

Rancour never feared that his brethren might interrupt his daily walks. He was the only man in the Alsandair who enjoyed the feel of grass between his toes, the scent of blooming flowers and the sight of the misty, rolling hills. His solitude was one more reminder that he was living a life foreign to his desire.

As he walked near the coast he listened to the ocean break against the rocks. Every sensation came to him, from the salty ocean spray to the tiniest blade of grass. Rancour had an extraordinary sense that kept him safe in case of spies.

"Brother!" he shouted when he smelled Kendil behind a tall,

grassy rock.

Kendil laughed and walked out into the open. "Forgive me impudence, but I was curious what you be doin'."

As the mist gently settled at their feet Rancour smiled. This was the only Alsandair he trusted, and he knew Kendil was not spying out of malice.

"I be thinkin', Kendil. When I walk along these paths I do so to clear me mind."

"Thinkin'?" Kendil asked as if the very word had a sour taste in his mouth. "You need to find a woman, brother, so that she can do the thinkin' for you."

"You are not angry then?" Rancour asked.

"Rancour, you 'ave kindness in your 'eart. An admirable trait to other clans per'aps, but for an Alsandair, 'tis a dangerous thing."

"I 'ave no fear o' death!"

"But do you fear the gods? They are the ones who will punish you should you not make a sacrifice."

Rancour thought about the men who had attacked them, and how the Alsandair had taken them prisoner. He also thought about the reasons why the men had attacked.

"They tried to save their children, just as you would 'ave tried to save me. What right do we 'ave to judge them guilty o' an action that we would 'ave done 'ad the situation been reversed?"

"They murdered one o' us!"

"They attacked with farm tools! They are not warriors. These men are no different than us. I spoke with them."

"Spoke with them? 'ow could you understand their gibberish?"

"They taught me."

"You spend too much time learning with your mind and 'eart. You speak with the animals too, do you not? Yet you do not mind them on your plate! Give these men to the gods for their plates, just as you would an animal to your stomach."

"There is a difference, Kendil."

"Man understands the evil he is. That is the difference." Rellik stared hard at the painting as he rolled onto his side. He could only meet the portrait's gaze for a moment before he sat up and smothered a shout. Memories! There was no escape from them, no running from them, and sometimes there was no forgiveness from them.

"How can you treat us with such malice? Have you no kindness in your heart?"

Rancour stood on guard outside the the cave where the prisoners were locked. Only days ago the words from these men had sounded like no more than guttural utterances, the same as any beast from the land. But it had not taken long before Rancour learned the villagers' tongue as easily as his own.

The prisoner said, "You seemed interested enough yesterday to learn our tongue. You have an incredible mind, friend."

"It be me curse, and don't call me friend!" Rancour turned on the man, bearing grit teeth and throwing a fist at the bars. When the prisoner shrank away Rancour calmed. In a near whisper he said, "Aye, I understand you. Please leave me be, I do what I do because the gods command it."

"You follow false gods then. Why would a god create such beauty if he wanted men to spoil it?"

"'Tis not me duty to question."

"Serve a god that says you must serve others. Do not question, seek."

Rancour faced the two men within the prison. One sat weeping on the floor while the other who spoke stood grasping the bars. He said again, "Seek."

"I would 'ave to leave me clan, me life. I cannot."

"You cannot lose what was never yours." He reached through the bars and grasped Rancour's shoulder. "But whatever you choose know this: I forgive you."

A voice from behind startled Rancour, "If it is your wish to set these men free, I shan't stand in your way." It was Kendil, his brother. "But if you do this you must say farewell to the Alsandair and never return."

"Farewell? For what?" Rancour turned to face his kin. "You are me clansmen. I will not turn away to save these innocents."

They stood before one another, Kendil wearing his best sword as did Rancour.

"Innocents? Sooner or later your words will see you 'ang on the gallows. You do not belong 'ere, brother."

"You would banish me?"

Kendil turned his back to his brother, and staring into the rising sun, he said, "You never belonged to us. 'Tis not the way o' an Alsandair to show mercy."

"And is that all we are? Mirror images o' one another?"

Kendil laughed. "Still you pose such questions on me. Rancour, my dear, kind brother, I will let you do this deed, but only if you vow on your honor that you will not return."

"Are you that ashamed o' me?"

Kendil, his body silhouetted by a crimson horizon, turned back to his brother. "I love you that much. Enough to know that the gods meant you for greater things."

"The gods? What madness there is in such belief! If they be

real, would they not ask, nay, demand! us to love one another?"

"You will not find that demand 'ere, Rancour. Especially…" Kendil fell short, suddenly unable to meet his sibling's gaze.

"Especially? You can tell me."

"I 'ave seen you change," Kendil whispered, still without meeting his brother's gaze.

Rancour turned away. "I know not what you mean."

"For what would the gods 'ave granted you such power, and such mercy, if they 'ad meant you to live your life as one o' us?"

"And what o' you? Did the gods mean you for this bane? Let us both flee this evil in which we live."

"Nay. Me blood dances when it spills another. 'Tis only yours that mourns."

"Ansgar will kill you should you stay."

"I will bear to them false witness. I shall say that you put a spell on me."

"And if the Council does not believe you?"

"Then I shall die." Kendil placed his hands on Rancour's shoulder and whispered, "I was born Alsandair, and it would be wrong of me to die anything but."

"So this means…."

"Farewell, dear brother." Kendil embraced Rancour and sighed. "Take with you this." Slipping a ring from his finger Kendil placed it in his brother's hand.

"This be your wedding band! What would your woman think should she not see it on you?"

"She cares not for me as I 'ave no love for 'er. It should be worn for love, and you, Rancour, will find that love. Go now before 'tis too late."

Rellik opened the box and took out his brother's band.

He remembered his indecision that day, and the fear he could not overcome. How could he leave the only life he had known to venture into a world he did not understand?

Most of all, he recalled what he had seen when he returned, too afraid to leave the only people he knew as family. The only place he could call "home."

Ansgar, standing on the gallows, pushed Kendil to the ground. He glared at his son and sighed, brushing a hand through his hair. First he shouted to his son, "You were in charge, Kendil!" and then to his people: "My kinsmen, you 'ave come this dawn to witness our gods' vengeance. But what it is that we 'ave found is the betrayal o' one o' us. We 'ave war ahead, and t'would do us much imprudence to engage our enemy before we 'ave appeased the gods."

"'ow are we to appease the gods without sacrifice?" shouted a clansman.

Kendil looked at his kinsmen, then at his father. "Ansgar, 'tis not me fault! Rancour put a spell on me that made me 'elpless."

Ansgar turned to the village who had gathered at the gallows. Drawing his sword he raised it to silence them and said, "My people! The escape is not me son's burden, but that o' 'is brother. Do not blame Kendil for this travesty, lest you shall feel the wrath o' mine steel!"

"But we came for a sacrifice!" called another voice.

"And so shall there be one," Ansgar brought the tip of his sword to rest on his son's neck, "I give you Kendil o' the Alsandair. We be not a clan that blames our kin, but we be one that dies for our corruption."

The crowd cheered so loudly with approval that a rumble from heaven went unnoticed. But what did not go unheard was a voice that said, "Corruption? What do you know o' this?"

They turned to the cave where, standing upon its roof, Rancour stared at them. Silence again took hold over the clan.

"Brothers! What be this madness? Are you so blood-thirsty that you would sacrifice an innocent man in place o' two men who only wished to right your wrong-doing?"

"You must be as daft as you are weak," Ansgar snarled.

"Daft? Is it not you who is about to 'ang your son, only because he let me free people who acted no different than you would in their place?"

"Rancour, you confuse self-righteousness for honor. Did you not participate in the slaughter? Do you now believe that because you set two free that you are absolved of the six you murdered?"

Rancour sighed, and looked at each of his kinsmen. In their eyes he saw himself and found his destiny in their damnation. "I do not know. Per 'aps I shall never escape the evil within me."

"I can tell you what makes this man unlike us," Kendil spat. "Rancour, you 'ave already escaped our evil. This clan wonders what it is that makes you unlike us? Simply this: Unlike the Alsandair, this man hates the sin within him."

"Kendil is under a spell again!" This time the unknown voice was softer.

"Nay, I see truth for the first time since I opened mine eyes as a babe. And 'tis 'cause o' that vision I know me brother is absolved o' our sin."

Ansgar laughed. "Then we shall put such virtue to a test. We shall kill but one man, and you, Rancour, shall decide which."

Rancour bit his lower lip and stared at the sky. His brow furrowed as he whispered, "Then I shall surrender my life. Set mine brother free."

"Nay! 'Tis I who should die," Kendil said.

Rancour leaped from where he stood and ran to the gallows. He stood before his brother and smiled. "Would it be anything less than just for us to die together? Let us both go to that Other World, and see what honor waits for us there."

Kendil took his brother's hand. "Then we die together, as it should be. If kindness be a sin, I take its punishment gladly. Thank you for finding that virtue in me."

"Then we meet our end with honor."

But though it was an end for Kendil, there was no such escape for Rancour. Rancour had spent a week on the gallows, swinging next to his brother's lifeless body, the memory of his brother choking echoing in his mind. When at last his kin came to release him, to bind him in shackles and take him to his father's tent, he went without a fight.

As Ansgar paced inside the tent, his muscles tensed like rocks. "I cannot understand the likes o' you. I trained you to be one o' us. Why then do you deny what I 'ave taught?"

Outside, two armed guards barred the tent's entrance, and throughout the village Rancour's clansmen waited for the sentencing of the first man to have survived the gallows.

"'Tis not me birthright. I was never one o' you. Not in mind, not in spirit, not even in ancestry."

"Did Kendil tell you we stole you from another clan?"

"Nay, 'e did not. 'e did not 'ave to."

"You are Rancour o' the Wulfsign, not Alsandair." Ansgar spoke softer this time. "What I tell you is truth. I stole you from a village o' demons."

"Tell me of them."

"It was during our spring move. The land we 'ad settled the previous autumn no longer provided food, and so we sought fertile ground. We came upon a valley where we could 'ave settled for generations, but we 'ad first to drive out a clan that was already settled. The Alsandiar 'as never been defeated in war, be for that one battle. But these were not men we fought. These were demons that could turn to a wulf at will."

Rancour rubbed the shackles that bound his wrists to his ankles. Thoughts about the week he spent hanging were no more than a blur, and he wondered how his life could have changed so fast. *"Demons? They were my kinsmen."*

"In the confusion o' battle, as the Alsandair fled for the first time in our existence, I 'appened upon an infant. I stole 'im, that is I stole you, and raised you as one o' us."

"To learn our weaknesses … to exact revenge?"

"To bring your power into our blood-line. What I 'ad not counted on was that you would bring us your weakness."

"Is kindness a weakness? Is mercy a weakness? Is virtue a weakness?"

"It is when you are an Alsandair!"

"And I was nothing more to you then?"

"Even less since you set our prisoners free."

"I cannot 'elp it! They 'ad done nothing to us!"

His loud outburst rang throughout the village, but was lost in his father's ears. Ansgar could no longer look at him and answered, *"I do not understand you. You could change into the wulf, break your bonds, even kill us all should you despise us so. Why would the gods 'ave granted a man like you such power?"*

"Per'aps they knew I wouldn't use it. I ask you again, what

will you do with me? A man who shall no longer live as you 'ave taught?"

"I shall banish you. All you are is a failed trial. You are not me son. Your sword shall stay 'ere, to be given to one o' me flesh."

"You would leave me defenceless?"

"Defenceless? You are more powerful without a sword than any mortal is with!"

"I will not use mine power that way."

"Then I will leave you with a sword crafted by your kind, per'aps even by your father. You shall be banished for your mercy."

"And this time I shall leave. This time I shall be free."

Ansgar laughed. "Free? You shall be damned by our memory. You shall never know freedom!"

Rellik looked to the heavens, praising God for having it in His will to banish him from the Alsandair. And he begged for it to be in His will for him now to find a place that he could call "home." He stared at his wedding band the same way he had at his brother over a millennium ago. He closed his eyes, wishing he could find a part of that identity still in him.

Wondering if he could complete his mission without it.

• • •

Jack sat on a hard wooden chair, hunched over his register, reading the anonymous entries with child-like pleasure. Light from the neon letters "OTEL" shone through his window, igniting Minitaw's outskirts like a full moon in a starless sky. He laughed, partly at those who petitioned to have him shut down, but mostly at those who partook in what his girls sold.

The door to his office opened, its one rusted hinge squeaking, stealing Jack's attention. At first he saw no one and figured the wind had blown it open, but as he rose he saw a bluish mist coming inside, followed by a tall stranger. He appeared young, with tight cheeks, deep brown eyes, and a short, neatly styled haircut. But he walked with the confidence of a man who had come to terms with his demons. Men like this never frequented his establishment.

But a sale was a sale.

"Lookin' fer a good time?"

The stranger turned to him and smiled, his eyes narrowing in such a way as to make him look devious.

"A good time?" he replied. "I live for pleasure."

"Then ye've come to the right place. Naomi'll be free, well, available that is, in a half hour." Jack grabbed a cigarette from an open box on the counter and lit up. Laughing, he added, "Maybe sooner."

"How revolting! I take no pleasure from the flesh. Nor do I understand your need to fill your lungs with that crap."

"So what do you want?"

The stranger chuckled. "A room."

"Nobody comes here fer a room, 'cept by the hour."

The stranger leaned over the counter and stared into Jack's eyes. As he spoke his pupils dilated and his voice sounded like a mother comforting a baby, "I'll tell you what does not give me pleasure: this conversation. Do not make me find pleasure in your death, friend. Tell me you have a spare room and that it is free."

"I have a spare room and it is free."

"Good. Now hand me its key and write my name in the

register: Shay Jackson."

"Shay Jackson."

"And remember my name, friend. It is a name that I have gone by for over one thousand years, and shall go by for ever after."

Jack reached behind himself, grabbed a key, and handed it to Shay. Then, after the door creaked open and closed, he returned to the register, unsure of what had just happened. Shrugging, he chuckled at the anonymous names and stared upon the first real one to ever cross his vision.

Shay threw his bag onto the bed and sat in a soft-cushioned chair. He sighed long and loud, looking at the water-stained floral wallpaper and shag carpet. He leaned over to the dresser, opened the drawer, and saw a Bible.

"How predictable these humans are," he groaned.

There was a time when he, too, was just as predictable. A time when he lived every day the same as the one before, a time before he learned the value of having an enemy.

Alas, those were times in need of change.

As Shay lay back on his bed, he stared up at his stone ceiling. The woman with whom he'd spent the night, whatever her name, gathered her clothes and stormed to the doorway, stopping only when she saw a man on the other side about to enter.

"Naztar, your brother is a fool!"

"A fool? Imagine such a thing. A vampyre who treats others with disrespect. Tisk, tisk."

"I never!"

"Stop by my chambers later and you shall."

Without another word she stormed past Naztar, who laughed in the wake of their conversation. He entered the room.

"Shay, how many more will you chase away? I mean, 'tis one thing not to enjoy taking her virtue, but she departed with all her blood! You, my friend, need to get drunk."

"Is that all there is to being a vampyre? Party all night, sleep all day, and get drunk on human blood?"

"Is that not enough?"

"I need more. Did you see the look on her face, in her eyes, when I told her to leave? She was crushed! That, my brother, was pleasure!"

"That? What did you do?"

Shay rose from his bed and walked to his bureau. Opening a drawer he took out a pair of purple tights and a yellow tunic.

"I ruined her day. I brought her misery! How fleeting is murder, but how much longer her hatred of me shall last in her heart."

"Shay, as ruler of the Kith I cannot allow you to make the other vampyres and blood slaves miserable. We live for pleasure. We all live for pleasure."

"I cannot find it here, Naztar. I will leave the Kith and find my pleasure out there. Somewhere."

"In the sunlight?"

"'Tis only legend that it can kill us."

"'Tis no legend that it shall lessen your power."

"I can stand a slight loss of power. T'would be worth it to find someone whose life I can ruin so terribly that he is outdone by his hatred for me."

"And I will out-do you, Rancour of the Wulfsign," Shay whispered to a clock on his motel room wall. "I will consume your soul with hatred."

CHAPTER 6

As Alix scanned the order of her classes for Day Two on the timetable she had posted on the inside of her locker door, she had all but forgotten the bizarre night of the party. First period she had Lit, second she had Math. She wondered what excuse she'd use when Miss Whelps asked her to write the homework on the board.

Alix turned back to her locker. The weekend had passed without incident, at least for her. There was news of another wolf attack on Friday, and grabbing her copy of Hamlet and her algebra book, she recalled her horrific apparition. Her jacket got in the way when she closed her locker door.

Then a voice said: "Hey rude-baby!"

Alix jerked and spun. The surprise broke her trance and sent her heart racing, but it was only Betty. Betty of the "embrace with Kharl", Betty. Closing her eyes she calmed down and told herself not to show her jealousy. "Hi."

Betty threw her long, dark hair back. "So what happened to you on Friday? Why have you been screening my calls?"

"I think I blacked out. I thought I was outside, then suddenly I was at home." She tried to say this as calmly as possible. "You can thank your friends for spiking my beer."

"They were only fooling around, baby." There was a pause. Then Betty sighed and added quickly, "I heard you saw Kharl and me in the kitchen."

Alix felt her face turn warm and hoped she wasn't turning red.

"What if I did?" she said as calmly as possible.

"We were just goofing around. It wasn't what it looked like."

"Whatever," Alix said trying not to sound like she cared.

"You worried us, y'know. Lara and Lenny were found dead. Totally ripped apart by a wolf."

"Lenny and Lara?" This time Alix knew she was turning red. Chills shot through her as she vaguely recalled how she'd seen a hog-tied corpse torn to pieces.

"Want better news? Guess who's asking you to the dance today?"

"Is it Kharl?" Alix smiled, glad to have changed topics.

"Yes!" Betty squealed. "Isn't it sweet? You have Kharl, I have Simon."

"What class do you have first?"

"Psych. Are we buying new dresses for Friday?"

"Would I put something old on this body?" Alix twirled and batted her eyelashes. "Fred's in your psych class, right?"

"The geek has an A plus, too. Why do you talk to him?"

"He's sweet. Deliver a message for me, 'k?"

"I'm not talking to that dork!" Betty turned her back on Alix. "And if you want popularity you won't either!"

"C'mon, Betty! Tell him to meet me in the library at lunch."

Betty glanced back. "You owe me big time, girl."

Minutes that day passed as though Father Time had fallen into a deep slumber. Ten minutes into Math, even after Miss Whelps's emotionless voice had lulled her into near unconsciousness, one disturbing thing swayed her from succumbing to slumber: Lenny really was missing from class. And until today, Lenny had boasted of a perfect attendance record since kindergarten.

"I need a volunteer. Who'll put number five on the board?" Miss Whelps always sounded like a mare caught in a barbed wire fence when she asked for a volunteer. It was the only time her voice didn't sound like a droll engine. She scanned the room with eyes as piercing as a raven's, until they landed on ... "Simon! Simon, come up here and put number five on the blackboard."

"I didn't understand number five."

"Then do as much as you can."

Simon looked at Alix and started for the board. When he slapped Kharl's hand, she knew he was up to something, but was just glad the teacher hadn't called her.

"Miss Conway," so much for luck, "number six?"

"I didn't finish the homework."

"And why not?"

"I didn't understand it."

"Then I better see you in here Thursday morning."

"I have ... home obligations."

Miss Whelps shook her head. Just as she was about to lace into her about priorities, Simon returned to his seat. "I'll speak with you later, Miss Conway." She turned to the board. "Now then ... who did number five?"

Simon couldn't conceal his smile. "That would be me."

"All you did was write the number five."

"That's all I understood, and just so you know, I have

football practice Thursday mornings."

As Miss Whelps preoccupied herself with Simon, a girl beside Alix threw a note on her desk. Large black lettering on the front read: "ALIX," and opening it she read:

"Meet me by the dumpsite at lunch. It's important.

Kim Q."

Alix folded the note and stuffed it into her binder, glancing at the clock. Another thirty minutes of class remained, and she wondered what Kim wanted. Should she bring Kharl in case there was trouble?

When at long last the school bell rang, Alix hurried to join the mad rush of students. She fought her way against traffic, away from the cafeteria, toward the exit. Once outside she walked to the dumpster, finding Kim waiting.

"Hi, Kim. I got your message, what's up?" She did her best to sound casual but stayed alert to her surroundings.

Kim sighed, rolled her eyes and turned stone cold. "Look, Blondie, I don't have some posse waiting to kick your ass. But my brother is going to fight Kharl today."

"Oh?"

"Look, I'm making a stand. You can either make one with me or stay a Barbie doll forever."

"What are you going to do?"

"Embarrass some sense into him."

Kim stared at Alix. A long silence ensued until Kim said, "Be a sheep then," and stormed off.

Fred, his face buried inside a WWII history book, waited for Alix in the library. He sighed, his thoughts drifting to

Betty and away from his book. She'd looked so beautiful when she spoke to him in class today ... he couldn't believe she spoke to him! He sighed again, and his glasses slipped down the slope of his nose. Catching them with his middle finger he pushed them snug against his brow and looked up to see Alix.

"Hi," he said, indicating with a sweep of his hand that she should sit in the chair next to him.

"Hi, Fred. Thanks for meeting me."

"You look worried. What's up?"

"I had the oddest thing happen this weekend, and I don't know what to make of it."

As Alix unfolded the events of Kharl's party and black out she avoided Fred's analytical gaze. She picked up a book from the table, flipped through the pages, and though she tried not to, she periodically met his eyes. Fred listened intently, trying not to look hurt that he wasn't invited to the party. When she finished, Fred just stared at her through his thumbprint-stained glasses. He took them off, and after wiping them with his tie, he put them back on and asked, "Is there anything special going on in your personal life? With Kharl, perhaps?"

Alix frowned. "Y'know, all you did was smudge them more." Taking Fred's glasses, she cleaned them. Quietly she answered, "Nothing's happening ... not really. Though I did see him kiss Betty."

"All right then..." Fred's face turned red. "Did you eat anything substantial, or different, before going to bed?"

She gave him back his glasses and shook her head from side to side.

"Is there anything going on with school? Home?" He sounded desperate now, searching for a logical explanation.

She suddenly smiled and her face glowed. "Sam's re-opening the store! He's trying to quit drinking!" Pausing she added, "But he still came home loaded last night."

Fred relaxed his thinker pose and slouched in his chair, as if relieved that logic could answer everything. "Alix, it's all very simple." He emphasized his words with chopping movements with his right hand. "Your blackout was a dream. Obviously it's symbolic of this change in your life, the murdered body being your fear that your father will fail."

"But Lenny and Lara really were killed."

Fred's face drew tight. "A pure coincidence. You probably added the details after you heard about them."

But I didn't hear about them until this morning! Alix thought.

Fred pushed his glasses up his long, thin nose. "Forget about it. You have a wonderful opportunity ahead of you. Don't let this weird circumstance take that away. Do all you can for your father."

"Thanks. I guess you're right."

"Anything else I can help you with?"

Betty, leaping into the private conversation, slammed a chair between them. She sat in it backwards, completely oblivious that she had interrupted Fred, and stayed silent. Though by her pursed lips it was obvious she forcibly held back some incredible news. She stared, her eyes wide and the ends of her lips curled into a smile.

Alix first took a discreet gander at Fred before rushing into Betty's game. He had never spoken of his affection, nor would he ever admit to it. But Alix knew. She also knew he was wasting his time if he thought he'd wait until Betty realized the sexiest muscle of all was the one within a man's head and not his throwing arm. He tried desperately to remain calm and relaxed, but his face was burning to the point where his nose turned purple. He tapped his foot but still looked into Betty's eyes while most boys stared elsewhere.

"What's the news?" Alix asked, saving Fred from further humiliation.

"Kharl and Derrick are ready to fight in Dead Man's Alcove!" Betty nearly burst as she sprang from her chair. She pulled Alix's arm to make her come, without waiting for a response, and Alix looked at Fred apologetically. He'd never be enticed into going with them. Not even his crush on Betty was enough to take him away from his principles. "Alix! Hurry!" Betty said in a harsh whisper, sensing her friend's hesitation. Then she noticed Fred and replied in disgust, "He can come too."

Betty never used his name when she spoke of Fred, not even when she spoke to him. With that insult Fred regained colour in his cheeks, buried his narrow face deeply into the center of a book and replied, "Alix, I refuse to be swayed into witnessing such barbarous actions."

Betty looked at him while mouthing the word: "loser" and, tightening her grip on Alix's arm, she asked, "Coming?"

Fred kept his face buried deeply in his book.

"I'll see you later?" she asked, rising from her chair.

Fred raised his face and pushed his fallen glasses up his nose. He smiled and nodded to let her know she had nothing to prove. No matter what, he'd always be her friend. Then

Alix followed Betty to where the fray was about to happen. The place that Rellik had deemed as his turf.

Dead Man's Alcove.

Alix stood beside Kharl, holding his arm at center stage for the whole school to see. Her mind was racing, wondering when Kim was going to make her move. More so, Alix wondered, what was she personally prepared to do? Was she willing to sacrifice having the star football hero for a boyfriend? She wondered where Kim was.

Alix swayed and suddenly had to catch her breath.

"You okay?" Betty asked as she caught her arm.

Alix felt light-headed and the world started to darken. She closed her eyes, and when she awoke…

She was a woman dressed in sackcloth living inside a drafty wooden cabin. Alix poured steamy water into two bowls and placed them on the table, one before a cloaked stranger and one before herself. His hood, catching his long, dark hair like a valley would a waterfall, lay around the back of his neck, and his rigid jaw reminded her of the rocks that built a slope to its peak. Her heart beat faster, but at the same time his soft gaze relaxed her. His eyes, whenever they looked upon her, moistened.

He cupped his hot bowl, neither flinching nor backing away from the pain. Lifting it toward his lips he leaned into it, sniffing its aroma like a beast would a fresh kill. When he drank he did so as if to extinguish a fire within his stomach, finishing it in only two gulps. The girl wondered, as he returned the bowl to the table, why she had let such a frightening person into her home.

But when he sighed and met his eyes with hers, she knew.

"You have lost someone dear to you?" she asked.

"Aye, that I 'ave."

He rose and turned his back to her. His squared shoulders slumped, and the head he held so high fell. He sighed again, this time wrapping his arms tightly around his chest as if to block any more pain from escaping. The girl bit her lip and considered for a moment what to say. He turned to her and when their eyes again met she knew in her heart they needed one another. Their meeting was not so much chance as it was fate.

"You could call my abode 'home' if you wish."

He smiled, his gesture meaning so much when it came so awkwardly to him. "T'would please me much. Your kindness would please me."

She rose and shot him a frown. "I ask only because my family was taken by the fever and I need help with the land. You, Sir, may sleep in the barn."

He was still smiling, and when he saw her do the same he said, "With th'other beasts. 'ow appropriate."

The girl smiled back and motioned to his bowl. "Would you fancy another?"

"Nay, but I thank you. What I fancy is sleep. I bid you farewell till the morrow."

He turned and walked out the door without waiting for her to respond. The girl stared after him, wondering in what strange adventure she had found herself.

"ALIX!" Betty shouted as Alix looked about herself in angst. She was no longer a woman in sackcloth, no longer in a cabin, and no longer serving a hooded stranger. To Kharl, Betty said, "Kick his butt!" Then to Alix, "Are you okay?"

"Yeah. I guess." But Alix knew she was not.

Alix rubbed the bottom of her nose and stared at Betty, wondering if she really did want to become like her. Was popularity, attention from boys, and a party-filled last year of high school worth sacrificing her morals? Shaking off those thoughts she turned her attention to the ensuing battle, feeling a sense of déjà-vu. She was still unsure if she would help Kim or not.

Derrick stormed into the alcove, as though he were a prize-fighter for his title bout. His six friends followed close on his heels with Kim struggling to get near her brother. Alix stayed where she was.

Kharl pushed Derrick and said, "Ready to have your other hand broken?"

"You're dead!"

"Wagon burner!"

"Enough!" Kim's voice cast everyone into silence. Derrick faced his sister.

"Kim, go home or stay silent, but don't embarrass me."

Kharl laughed. "I always knew you needed a woman to do your fighting."

Everyone started laughing. Kim refused to move and said, "Are you going to hit me too?"

Derrick glared hard at his sister. "You're a disgrace."

"Derrick!" Kim shouted after him as he stormed from the alcove. She looked at Alix, frowned, and said, "You Barbie dolls are all the same," before she chased after her brother.

Kharl was about to say something to the crowd when he heard, "Sir, if you might excuse me, I'd like to get to my locker."

This guy was tall, thin, and had no sign of muscle. He had short blonde hair and brown eyes that made him look peaceful rather than intimidating. He looked becoming sporting a mahogany pin-striped suit. Only Kharl remained unimpressed, and holding his ground he beamed hard into his adversary's eyes. The newcomer had let his back-pack drop to the ground. At first Kharl thought this guy wanted to fight, but fear whitened the guy's features as he straightened his tie and vest.

The stranger, baring his bright teeth in a smile, said beneath his trembling voice, "Perhaps I should introduce myself. How rude of me. I am Shay Jackson. Now, if you will pardon me. Please."

Kharl almost laughed. Puffing out his broad chest to dwarf him with his bulk he pushed the stranger.

"Sorry, pal. This here is Dead Man's Alcove. Nobody uses these lockers."

"How odd ... I pray you will tell me then: if they are not to be used, why have them?"

Kharl tensed his muscles and puffed himself out. "For fighting."

If nothing else in the jock's attitude gave provocation to fight then the look on his face should have been enough in itself. And it was. Shay lashed out, grabbed Kharl by the throat and lifted him off the ground. The crowd stepped back, shocked at the ease with which the stranger had lifted their prized football star.

"Do you wish to fight me?" Shay asked with a cool serpent's breath, yet never losing his hint of charm.

This guy's grip was like iron and Kharl wished the whole

school wasn't watching. Gasping desperately for air, he tried to say "no" before his eyes lolled into the back of his head, but no sound came from his constricted throat. He managed to only mouth the word.

When the stranger appeared satisfied with his submission he released him, letting the jock fall hard onto the floor. Stepping aside to allow Simon enough space to pick him up and get him to the school nurse, he bowed.

As if they were mice scampering lost in a maze, the students went on about their usual duties, no one staying to question, nor even welcome, this new stranger. Betty grabbed Alix and stopped her from following the crowd.

"Let's welcome the new guy."

Alix smirked. "I don't think so."

"Oh, sure. Yesterday, you're 'Miss Welcome Wagon' but today you're a prude!"

"Am not! He just spooks me."

"And Rellik spooked me."

When the stranger noticed the two of them still standing inside the alcove, he sank into another bow, this time for only them. Alix grabbed Betty firmly by the arm and dragged her away, noticing that Rellik was entering the alcove.

The tall stranger, still deep in his bow after the two girls had left, did not rise in Rellik's presence.

"Give it a rest, Shay," Rellik said in an ancient Gaelic tongue. Then he said with a deep throaty growl, "I wondered when you'd come."

"How kind of you to think of me, my friend!" Shay responded in the same language, rising to stand at his full height. Rellik turned to fiddle with his lock as Shay marched up and down the alcove, studying each locker as though the one he chose was the most important decision of his life. Then, opening the one beside Rellik's, he studied its interior.

"It's her second life, my friend," the vamp's voice echoed from inside the locker. "I would not risk losing her twice."

Shay poked his head out to face Rellik, who had turned crimson.

"You don't love her! When I left my clan she was my whole world."

"Then it was your mistake to think that no one else would compete for her love."

"Love? Was it love that…."

The tall stranger laughed, cutting Rellik short. He remained calm, took out a red binder from his knapsack, and, placing his bag in the locker, he closed the door. He then took out a lock and secured it, taking his time to turn to Rellik, who stood right up against him. Shay looked down to meet the angry glare and spoke so his voice would also sound like a deep growl, but unlike Rellik he never lost his hint of charm.

"When last I saw her she was still alive."

"You partook in evil."

"And you have to catch me before you can convict me. Or have you not yet accepted the burden of being a were-wolf? You are not without hardship, nor are you without commandments. Commandments separate your kind from mine. Obtain her love freely and you will be given mortality. I call that a curse, but what do you call it? Would you give up living forever for love?"

"You do not love her. You do not understand."

"Was it love that made you kill her, Rancour the Wulfsign?"

Rellik grabbed the vamp and slammed him against the wall. The Wulfsign puffed out his impressive muscular form and growled, "I will win her 'eart. Just as I won it a millennium ago."

The tall stranger rolled his head back in a fit of laughter. He brought his gaze to meet Rellik's glare and made clear his intent to dominate the shorter man with his height.

"Watch that accent, friend. You are no longer 'Rancour the Wulfsign, once o' the clan Alsandair'. Do not forget the rules pertaining to gaining the love of those in their second life. She does not remember you, nor can you recall for her her first life."

"There will be no need. She will know my soul."

"Soul?"

"Once she gets to know me she will remember."

"Get to know you? How do you expect to remember sociability when you have spent so long in solitude?"

Rellik's eyes flashed crimson. "I have not been alone these past thousand years. I have been among your kind! Learning to defeat you."

"You are so unnerving! Help me, someone, I am so helpless!" Shay laughed. "You were not with my kind. You have been among Whittaker's renegade sect of vampires. You learned nothing."

Rellik turned his attention to his locker and said, "I suppose Indigo followed you."

Shay rolled his head back in another fit of laughter, wiping away non-existent tears to emphasize the joke he had found in Rellik's question. "Still upset about the last time I led him to you?"

Rellik grabbed his notebook from the locker's shelf and slammed the door shut. Though he had turned to meet Shay's stare, he did so this time so deeply that his voice bellowed into the vamp's mind: *"He shot up my car!"*

Shay smiled, appearing quite undaunted, though this time he hadn't laughed. "And you say nothing of the wound you took?"

Rellik was about to answer but, even though his muscled back faced the alcove's entrance, he could tell by Shay's familiar grin that Alix had returned. That damned grin angered him to no end, often making him wish for Shay's demise ... but rules were rules.

He heard Shay say, much too pleasantly, "Alas, but my heart has stopped! Pray someone tell me who is this lovely vision?"

"Irish dog! Why don't you go back to where ya came from?"

Ariana walked tightly beside Rancour through the crowded, narrow cobblestone streets. Many stared, few shouted, but all showed their disgust for him in some manner. She looked up at his rigid jaw, bushy low-lined eyebrows, and playful grin. He seemed completely undaunted by the remarks, as if he had not heard them.

"They do not bother you?"

"Why should they? I don't know them." And to him it was that simple. Or, could it be, she wondered, that as brawny as he was he was that much ill-equipped to fight? Is that why he was banished

by his people? Rancour pointed to a minstrel and laughed. His eyes widened and he hurried close. Closing his eyes he listened intently, each note sweet to his ear. Ariana was amazed by him.

"Have you not heard a lyre before?" she inquired.

"I 'ave not. 'ow does it work?"

But before she could explain, a tall, wide fellow stepped between them and the musician. He glared with blue eyes, chest heaving and muscles flexed. He stood with no more than a hair's width between he and the Wulfsign, a challenge thrown for all to witness. When he spoke his voice was harsh and controlled.

"We do not want your kind 'ere."

Rancour reached out to bring Ariana safely behind him. He met the gaze head on without blinking, but when he spoke he did so calmly. There was even a smile on his lips.

"I mean to show no disrespect, but I cannot 'elp the circumstance o' my birth any more than could you."

"I was born English by the will of God." The burly fellow did not back down. Several others stood behind him, urging him on.

Rancour looked pensive. "Then per'aps you would share your noble position with me by allowing me a life o' peace."

Silence. Both men glared at one another. Until finally the burly fellow laughed, and patting Rancour on the shoulder, he said, "He's all right! This newcomer is all right!"

The crowd dispersed and Rancour, as though nothing had happened, turned to Ariana and said, "A lyre you say?"

"Were you afraid you could not best him?" she asked though she knew better.

Rancour threw a coin at the minstrel and said, "There is no honor returning to a life I 'ave chosen to leave."

Ariana could not help herself. Standing on her tiptoes she kissed his cheek and said, "Wait here, I'll gather what we need from the market."

"Aye," he said caressing the moist spot on his face. He watched after her as she walked off into the crowd. He did not know exactly the words to describe the emotions he felt when with her. It was unlike anything he had known. His heart fluttered, his lips smiled and there was sorrow whenever she was not near. Was it love?

"What else could it be?" asked a man beside him.

"Pardon?" Rancour said and turned to face a tall, thin man.

"Your bravado, I witnessed everything. You are the bravest man I have ever met. Allow me to introduce myself, I am Shay Jackson." The tall man bowed. He was pale and quite sickly looking. It was as if he had not eaten in weeks.

"You are met well, friend. Might I ask, and forgive me impudence, if you are down on your luck?"

Ariana returned and said to the merchant, "Would you excuse us? I must speak with my hired hand a moment."

They walked away from the stranger, and when next Ariana spoke, she whispered: "What do you know of this man? I have heard that there was a murder in the hamlet last night, how do we not know…."

"Ariana! T'was not a murder, but a wulf attack. You cannot fault this man with superstition. Look at 'im. 'e is pale and does not look like 'e 'as eaten in days." Rancour picked her up and twirled her in the air. "I 'ave found me chance to show true honor! This merchant needs our aid, and I know that we don't 'ave the food to spare, but I will cut me own rations in 'alf…."

Ariana smiled. "Speak no more. You may welcome this stranger, but not to my home. Welcome him to our home. He will take your lodgings in the barn…."

"And I?"

"You will sleep in the house. With me. I am, after all, your angel."

Rancour turned back to the merchant who asked, "And who might this vision be?"

"This is Alexandria," Rellik answered coldly, no longer so young, nor so innocent.

Alix smiled when Rellik had taken it upon himself to introduce her, even if he hadn't turned to her while doing so. She added to Rellik's introduction, "And this is Betty."

Rellik didn't turn to face them, not even when Shay stepped around him.

"I am Shay. Shay Jackson." He beamed his pearly whites and a sparkle shimmered from his sunken, brown eyes. "Could one of you lovely ladies please show me to my history class? A Mister Pausron, it is."

Rellik cringed at the thought of Shay taking the same class as he.

Betty said, "That's my class! I'll show you where it is!" and wrapping her arm around his, she gave Alix a familiar glance. Alix didn't tag along.

Shay spoke a few incoherent words as they departed from the alcove. Rellik, with his back to Alix, smiled for the first time in centuries.

"Rellik?" Alix asked with a slight quiver in her voice. "Do you want me to show you where the class is?"

Her voice sang in his ears more beautifully than a chorus of songbirds. Her kindness hadn't changed in a millennium, and Rellik didn't know what he'd do if he lost her twice.

Rancour finished lighting the fire and walked to Ariana. He smiled, looked deeply into her eyes, and pulled her close to him. He thought briefly of his brother, of the love that Kendil had said he would find, and slipping a ring from his finger, he said, "I wish you to 'ave this."

As he handed her the wedding band Kendil had given him, he met her curious eyes.

"What be this?" she asked.

"'Tis me soul, Ariana. Wear it only if you want it."

She took it and smiled, leaning to him and kissing him deeply. As she took his hand in hers Ariana led him toward the bedroom. Rancour gently pulled her back.

"Nay, Ariana."

"'Tis all right. I love you."

"And I you more than life itself. 'Tis why I wish to wed you first."

She handed him back his band and said, "Then give this to me that day, Rancour. Give me your soul only when I can give you mine."

He took it back and vowed by his honor that they soon would wed, and gently kissing her he praised the heavens for his good fortune.

Knowing there would never be a time when he didn't need her, when his heart didn't feel empty without her.

"No. I can find it myself," Rellik answered, the words sounding foreign against the love he still felt for her. He wanted to take Alix's hand, to pull her close, and never let go. But as his vision hit the ground he walked past her, uncertain why he felt so afraid to open his soul once again.

CHAPTER 7

"The Alsandair hated me for the kindness that
I had shown our enemy, and they also hated my
brother for that which he had shown me. It would
not have mattered to my clan even if we had
gone on every day after that living the evil they
worshipped. We were now an abomination, because
we were not the same.

"And now I must wonder which the greater deed
was: my liberation of our prisoners, or Kendil who
had set me free?"

—Wulfsign

L ittle more than two years had passed since Sam last stepped inside "Conway Groceries," and just as he'd expected, the place was in desperate need of a harsh cleaning and restocking. He arrived early in the morning, even though his head pounded with a familiar beat and his dry throat pleaded for quenching. He'd neglected his health to ensure the store would be ready for reopening by mid-afternoon, but by late afternoon the shelves still had the same dust blanket, the refrigerators still had the same mildew and his new boxes of stock still remained unopened.

The only thing that Sam had found it in him to do was to flip his "closed" sign to the "open" position.

"Open for what?" he said aloud, knowing how much rode on this foolhardy decision of his. He wished he hadn't mentioned anything to Alexandria before he had found success, and, as though his wife were there in the grocery store with him, he said, "Trina, I so need you now."

He collapsed onto an unopened crate as though his strength rode on his whispered breath, and sinking his solemn face into his dry palms he prayed his daughter could forgive him twice.

At least he recalled where he had stashed his whisky.

The faint sound of the door opening and the once common song of the bell jingling hadn't reached his ears, but a few seconds later when footsteps neared he called out, "I'm sorry. Store's closed."

"I still expect to get paid," Rellik's raspy voice growled as his footsteps came to a halt.

Sam could have sworn he heard something snap from deep within him. He wasn't sure why that remark had bothered him so much, but as he rose to tower over the much shorter young man his rage grew beyond control. He felt his face blush a painful crimson, and when the young man met his angry stare head on with equal force, the show of contention only infuriated him more. Sam tightened his hands into clenched fists, opened them fast, and repeated this gesture several times.

"Listen to me and you listen good," Sam whispered beneath his harsh breath, "I don't know who you think you are, but you work for me and you will address me with respect!"

"If you do not open the store, then I work for no one."

Sam couldn't figure out why the anger in him burned, but the longer he stared at the teen the more he hated him. It was irrational and he knew that, yet it was as if he had stepped out of himself and watched helplessly as the fury took over. Sam rammed his index finger into Rellik's chest and pushed.

"Get out. Out of my store! And out of my home! I don't know what kind of mind games you play, but they end right here!"

Rellik knew it would be best to leave. He wasn't afraid, after all Sam was only mortal and should he choose to strike he could easily be subdued. But Sam's suffering was not unlike looking into a mirror image, a reflection of one who has lost a loved one. Rellik had seen the urn of ashes beneath the portrait when he'd been in the den for his interview. He found it discomfiting to watch someone else handle his loss in the same manner as he did: by driving those who might care for him as far away as possible. Yet even in his worst time of despair, he had found kindness.

Rellik wanted to leave, but knew he could not. This mortal did not have long to wait until his life would end, and without compassion Rellik knew that Sam would waste away his days.

"Please forgive my impudence. I meant you no disrespect. If you wish me to depart then I shall. But from the look of your store it appears you are in great need of aid." He made a sweeping motion with his hands at the scattered boxes.

"Would you listen to yourself? Even your apology sounds condescending! You have no right to judge me! You don't know what I lost!"

Rellik shook his head and turned toward the door. Self-pity had taken too strong a hold over Sam for reason to reach him.

"Do you truly believe that no one's loss is equal to your own? Are you so lost in that demon's drink that you believe the loss of your wife has earned you the pity of the world? My pity is extended to your daughter. For not only has she lost a mother, but a father as well."

The mention of Alexandria released the grip of madness from Sam. His temper cooled and he realized that the anger was not from this kid's attitude but from a need ... no, desire ... to drink. He slumped back down onto an unopened crate and answered, "I'm sorry, Rellik. I do need your help."

Rellik turned the "open" sign to read "closed," grabbed a broom, and set to work.

CHAPTER 8

Several hours after the sun had set Kharl lay upon a picnic table with his gaze locked on the starry sky. The moon, unlike the sun who offered earth its warmth, stole away the heat and shrouded the world in surreal light. It called upon thousands of specks to rejoice in its rule, but night did not completely belong to the moon. For as the angels came, they streaked the heavens with white, green, pink and gold, setting Kharl's thoughts ablaze. The northern lights brought him back to a time of innocence when he believed he could hear sprites singing to the beat of the dark, angelic dance.

Minitaw offered many places where he and his friends could let their imaginations roam, or more accurately, many places they could intoxicate their imaginations. Kharl took the last swig from the bottle Simon had stolen from his parents' liquor cabinet.

Simon and Betty lay together on the grass with their legs locked in a lover's hold. Their kissing was the only sound louder than the crickets.

Alix lay on the picnic table beside Kharl. She was close to him, her shivering body pressed tight against him. They both stared at the magical Heavens, each lost in their own world of contemplation. Kharl wasn't sure what to make of Alix; she just wasn't like other girls. Most of the time she seemed interested in him, but she didn't play the game quite as easily as, well, Betty. He reached for her hand and felt it go rigid. She even sounded like her breathing stopped, but slowly she relaxed and intertwined her fingers with his.

"You cold?" he asked her.

"I'm okay," she answered, not understanding his intent.

"You sure? 'Cause if you are, I could put my arm around you and keep you warm." He couldn't remember a time when he had to be this obvious.

"Uh, sure," Alix answered. She lifted her head as he swung his arm beneath her and pulled her closer. He hoped to get her face near his so he could kiss her, but she kept her gaze locked on the stars. It wasn't helping things, either, that Betty and Simon were practically screwing in the grass just yards away.

"Do you two mind?" Kharl shouted.

"We're only kissing," Simon shouted back.

"Whatever you're doing it's bugging me. Besides, with the amount of cops goin' by you're going to get caught."

Simon stirred, taking his gaze away from Betty. "What else is there to do? You finished the bottle we brought."

They all covered their eyes as another cruiser flashed its lamp at them and called, "You kids see anything?"

Kharl rose, fighting the urge to give them the finger. "No, we haven't. Maybe if you come back in two minutes instead of ten there'll be a dead body then."

"Don't get lippy, kid," the officer warned as he drove away.

"Well, I've certainly had it," Kharl said and hopped from the table. "Anyone else for Icy Shakes?"

He offered Alix his hand for support. She said, "Well, it's dark and cold. I didn't exactly dress for this wind, so I'm up for Icy Shakes."

"Icy Shakes it is," they all said in unison.

Simon and Kharl led as they walked down the highway, with Alix and Betty lagging behind. Betty asked, "What's your problem?"

"What?"

"What? What do you mean, 'what'? You got Kharl, baby. He's tall, handsome, and wanted by every girl in school. If you're not careful you're going to lose him."

Betty hurried to take her place beside Simon. He wrapped his arm around her waist and she kissed his cheek, glancing back at Alix.

Kharl lagged behind to let Alix catch up. He walked so close that he banged his shoulder into her, and their hands kept brushing until she let him catch hers. He was the boy that everyone wanted at school, and she knew she owed her popularity to his affection. Over the past few days she was seeing a side to him that she just didn't like. The fights, the arrogance, and the fact that she couldn't shake that image of him kissing Betty.

After a long, brisk walk the gang finally arrived at Icy Shakes. The warmth was welcome, and with a wave of their hands they signalled Bob to cook their usual.

"Hey kids," he shouted, throwing several patties onto his grill.

Icy Shakes was a popular place this brisk night. Fred sat at a table in the back, his nose engulfed in a textbook and a half eaten burger on a tray. He pretended not to notice the gang, but Alix saw his eyes peer over the book and quickly dart back down. Betty glared at her before the thought to invite him even entered Alix's mind.

Rellik had also come. He sat at a booth near the middle of the restaurant, his back to the front door and shoulder pressed against the glass window. He was dressed in his heavy leather coat and had on the dark shades that hid his eyes. No thoughts to invite him to sit with them entered Alix's mind, but she was curious to know how things had gone with Sam's store. Did he actually open it, or was Rellik here because Sam got drunk and gave up again? Not wanting her fears turned into reality, she chose to just ignore Rellik.

Kharl entered the seating area first and gave Rellik a hard glare as he passed by. He was still holding Alix's hand, and she felt a sharp pain as he tightened his grip for but a second. They sat in the booth directly behind him, with Kharl and Alix's backs to Rellik but both facing Fred.

Betty and Simon sat facing Rellik with their backs to Fred. They were acting so oblivious to Rellik's presence that it was obvious it bothered them. But all he did was wolf down his meal.

"Earth to Alix," Fred said, waving his hand over her eyes. She hadn't even noticed when he had walked to their table.

"Oh. Uh, hi, Fred." Alix didn't know what to say. Kharl and Simon were giving each other looks and nudges, snickering as they mimicked Fred's unique facial expressions.

"I'm going over to talk to Rellik," Fred said as he glanced at Kharl and Simon. Then straight at Alix he added, "I'm surprised you aren't curious about how things went at your dad's store."

"I'm curious! Maybe I just don't want to talk to the weirdo." She rolled her eyes at him, even though it made her feel awful to treat him like that.

Kharl said, "Maybe I should go over there and ask the freak how things went. He and I are due for a conversation."

"No!" Alix said far too quickly. "I mean, well, I am curious to know how things went tonight."

Alix inhaled deeply and got up. Kharl, Simon and Betty were all staring at her with grins that meant they expected her to somehow ridicule Rellik. If she really wanted in with this group she knew she'd better do it, but that would also mean including Fred in that ridicule. She wasn't completely sure what she'd just got herself into.

Following Fred she sat opposite Rellik in his booth and said, "Hi." She blushed, glad that Fred had sat beside her. "How – how was work?"

Rellik looked at the pair sitting across his table. His brow furrowed, and after he let out a long sigh. "It went well. Your father is a good man."

Rellik continued eating and Alix nudged Fred to leave. She'd got the information she needed and now she was done. But Fred cleared his throat and shoved his hand before the stranger. "I'm Fred."

Rellik looked quite thoughtful, but neither accepted nor offered his own friendly gesture. Fred took back his hand and rose from the booth. "You're welcome to join us," said Fred.

Then they left him alone and went back to their table. Fred took it upon himself to sit beside Betty.

Alix watched Simon's eyes dart around the room as fast

as his thumbs twiddled. She hoped that whatever Simon's insidious mind concocted it wouldn't concern Rellik. Kharl was glaring at Fred, and she wondered if he would keep his temper in check.

"Boy," Simon spoke just barely louder than his foot tapped, his devious character shattering Alix's hopes. "First that guy breaks up your fight, and now he moves his turf into your hangout. I hear he's telling everyone how he would'a kicked your ass if you hadn't chickened out."

"And just who is this 'everyone', Simon?" Fred sounded angry. "Consider first that he has no friends in Minitaw."

Alix knew how Fred figured out if Simon was telling a lie: by listening to his foot tap. Kharl turned red from a mixture of shame and anger, and Alix knew he was beyond reason. If only, she wished, Kharl knew when Simon was using him as bait for entertainment.

"Did you see the way he looked at me?"

"An amazing trait you have," Fred said as diplomatically as possible. "Wish I could tell someone's intent through dark sunglasses. An even more admirable one to see his look with your back to him."

"I'm gifted, alright? Why don't you go hang out with your other friends, you nerd? Oh, that's because you got no friends!"

Betty squealed at the prospect of another fight just as the kitchen bell rang. Fred took that jingle as a welcome escape, and very clumsily clambered out from the bench into the aisle. As Fred took his leave, Simon continued playing Kharl.

"So why don't you go teach him a lesson? Scared?"

Kharl breathed hard and glared at Simon. If it weren't for the fact that they'd been best friends for years he probably would have beaten him up. But instead he looked at Alix and said, "Baby, I got to go put that freak in his place."

She didn't want to move. She didn't want to see another fight, at least not one between Rellik and Kharl. But what she wasn't certain about was whether or not it was Kharl she worried about or if it was Rellik. Feeling Betty kick her from beneath the table and seeing her mouth the word, "Move" Alix slowly got out of the booth. Kharl spun to sit opposite Rellik.

Alix's heart leaped into her throat as she watched Kharl act on Simon's challenge. She wished she knew exactly what he intended to do and how Rellik would respond. She rubbed the bottom of her nose.

Rellik didn't appear to care one way or another. He just started on his second burger, drawing his breaths as timed, even strokes. Kharl acted just as calm and cool, leaning back in his seat. He spoke loudly enough so the rest of his gang could hear his bravado.

"So. You're a fighter?" Kharl chuckled before and after the word 'fighter'.

Rellik said nothing.

"Hey! I'm talkin' to ya, buddy."

Rellik suddenly looked up and glared, his shades glowing a dim hue of scarlet. Kharl looked behind him and saw Simon give him two thumbs up and Betty quivering with excitement. He looked to Alix, who was biting her upper lip.

"Are you giving me another mean glare, Rellik? Why don't we find out by taking off these shades."

Kharl reached for Rellik's shades, but Rellik sprang with lightning speed and grabbed the jock's wrist. As they stared at each other Kharl clenched his free hand into a tight fist. He waited for Rellik's next move. All the stranger did was let go, and sip the Coke that sat on the table.

"Get away from me," Rellik warned. "I'm eating."

Alix rose from her seat and sat beside Kharl.

"C'mon," she whispered so Rellik wouldn't hear, "leave him alone."

Rellik stopped eating. Alix looked at him and knew he was staring into her eyes through his dark shades. His furrowed brow lost its tension and the darkness in his features lightened. He obviously thought her a part of Kharl's foul plan and that saddened her.

"I'm not doing anything!" Kharl bellowed in defence. "I'm only trying to talk to the freak!"

Rellik smiled, and Alix knew he was aware of her innocence. The outsider said nothing and concentrated on his meal.

"That's it," Kharl mumbled. He acted quickly, throwing a punch aimed for Rellik's jaw, hoping to catch him off guard. But without any noticeable effort the stranger caught the punch with his free hand, and with his other, he continued to eat.

Tears welled in Kharl's eyes and his face distorted from Rellik's powerful grip. The outsider, heedless that his captive struggled in vain, finished his burger and slowly rose to stand. Rellik sneered, as if he wanted to break the jock's fist, but when he looked at Alix his demeanour lightened.

She again met his lonely gaze through the mirrored

glasses and somehow knew he held back from fighting for her. She almost wished he wouldn't. Rellik grabbed his sunglasses, but didn't remove them. Half-smiling, he released Kharl's hand without harm.

Kharl watched as the outsider shuffled from the booth to leave. Rellik's dark features bore no expression as he walked toward the exit, and after Kharl pushed past Alix to rush behind his enemy, he grabbed the new kid by the shoulder.

"I'm not through with you yet!"

Alix dashed behind Kharl, grabbed his shoulder and yanked as hard as she could.

"Leave him alone!"

"What's your problem?" the jock yelled, releasing Rellik and turning to Alix. Without realizing how close she stood he slammed into her and knocked her to the ground. Rellik stood perfectly still, keeping his back to Kharl, but when he heard Alix hit the ground, even though it had been an accident, he turned with the devil's scowl.

Rellik spun and side kicked his adversary squarely in the chest. A shout of air exploded from the jock's lungs as he hit the hard floor. Rellik waited for Kharl to move. He didn't. Then the outsider met Alix's eyes, sighed and turned, heading out the door without uttering a single word.

Alix chased after him without grabbing a jacket. The cool winds outside had grown stronger and chillier. Her teeth chattered from the cold, but she didn't want to lose him. Though she didn't know why.

"I'm sorry," she called, in hopes her voice might carry itself over the wailing winds. "My friends are all jerks."

Rellik didn't respond, nor did he slacken his brisk pace.

His wide shoulders tensed, his head bowed, and though he had tucked his hands within deep pockets she knew he clenched them into tight fists. Another charge of wind hit Alix, tearing through her thin silk shirt. She eyed his heavy leather jacket with envy, and wondered how much longer she could pursue him.

"C'mon, Rellik! I'm trying to be friends with you!"

He stopped. It appeared that her words had touched him, but he didn't say anything. He didn't even face her. She walked behind him and placed her hand on his shoulder.

"Look, I know you haven't been made to feel welcome. But then you haven't acted like you want to be either."

Still, he said nothing. In the darkness he slowly turned to face her, taking her hand into his. She shook from the cold … mostly, from the cold. The look on his face had become so intense that Alix wanted to hold him. He didn't smile when he at last let her hand free and she wondered what he was going to do. But this time the unknown brought no fright into her heart, and as the half-smile returned to his dark face she knew she was safe. He removed his leather jacket and placed it around her.

As Alix stood amidst the bitter wind her hair blew over her distraught face. With only a single fingernail she caught what hair had blown in front of her eyes and brushed it aside, staring after the stranger. She pulled Rellik's oversized jacket closer around herself, her hair blowing across her vision.

And she watched him leave, without a word, into the darkness.

CHAPTER 9

"I have been told by many people, usually by those who claim to be close to one deity or another, that to find true happiness one must stay away from all of Earth's pleasures. 'What,' I would implore, 'are these things which you deny?' Wealth, promiscuity and power over individuals, they tell me.

"It is those people for whom I feel the most pity. Not because they have denied themselves life's pleasures, but because they know not what pleasure is.

"When you love someone so much that even their imperfections move you, and they love you the same, that is when you learn true pleasure.

"And it is that very thing which is denied to one who lives for ever."

–Wulfsign

s Alix stood outside Icy Shakes, the cold wind
whistled in her ears and nipped at her nose. She'd lost
track of the time and wondered, as she pulled open the
restaurant door, if she would find her friends still inside. She
was not at all relieved when she did. Simon and Betty were
discussing "that psycho" while tending to Kharl's wound,
and it didn't appear that any of them recalled that Rellik
hadn't started the fight. Or that he had left so it would not
continue.

How convenient, she thought.

Betty leaped from her seat to Alix. "You're wearing that
freak's jacket? Look at what he did to your boyfriend!"

Alix bit her lip and rubbed the bottom of her nose. She
sighed and saw Fred sitting alone in another booth. She
drew from his strength and glared at Betty.

"Did you happen to notice what Kharl was doing? I've
had it with this peer pressure to be just like all of you!"

"Really? And whose friend are you now, the geek or
the freak?"

Alix slapped her hard and said coldly, "You're a bitch."

Simon jumped in the middle. "Whoa! I'm all for a cat
fight and all but this is one we'll all regret in the morning."

Betty never took her eyes off Alix. "Simon, move now
so I can kick her ass!"

"C'mon, Betty. Let's just sit and talk."

Betty turned her glare on him. When he wouldn't budge she grabbed her coat and stormed out. Simon turned to Alix, shook his head, and helped Kharl up. As they left Icy Shakes Kharl said to Alix, "This ain't over!"

Alix walked to Fred, who was grinning, as if pleased by the fall-out of her foray into popularity.

"Congratulations," he said.

Alix looked at him and smiled. "On what?"

"Freedom to make your own choices, for one. Did you really think you'd ever fit in with a bunch of robots?"

Fred pushed the tray of food he had set out before himself nearer her. On it was her usual cheeseburger and chocolate shake.

"I just wanted to know how it would feel to be like everyone else," she whispered.

He examined her thoughtfully and said, "He gave you his jacket. Can I assume you've made some progress?"

"No," she answered before picking at her burger. "And I don't know what to do anymore. He just left without saying a word."

"I must admit he frightened me earlier. He has such rage inside him that I don't think it's a good idea to put yourself in the middle of it. There must be something about his past that's making him act like this."

"Well, I give up," Alix said, a long sigh following.

"I think that would be best. The safest choice for us all."

Alix smiled and lifted her shake to her lips. Before taking a long sip of the cool liquid she said, "You talk funny, you know that?"

Fred, too, smiled. He took pride in how much she had grown since. She had truly become a better person since she no longer had her other friends as her sole influence.

His secret desire was that if he could create such a change in her, then perhaps he could create one in Betty. But that was doubtful. He may have had his eyes on her for what seemed like forever, but sometime during the summer she'd become Simon's girl. And, from what he'd heard, Simon had given her a lot more than just his heart. He wished she'd let him show her feelings genuine and real.

A hope that the torrential rains of reality slowly weathered away.

• • •

Rellik walked along the highway beside the woods. He was cold, physically and emotionally. Immortality shielded him from many things: disease, poison, death. But it did nothing against pain. As he fell into deep thought, as the bitter cold nipped at his immortal body, he concentrated on his form. He slowly contorted and shifted. His bones cracked and healed, his skin shed and grew, and his hair burned, replacing itself with thick, coarse fur. Rellik had become a white dire wolf, free to lose himself in a memory of long ago.

Rancour sat in a dark, musty tavern, absently looking about himself, slamming back drink after drink. He'd left Ariana alone with Shay, knowing it best not to share this night's thoughts with either mortal. Tonight he needed to forget the day's events, and he would have, if only alcohol would steal his inhibitions as it had everyone else's. He questioned why the gods allowed mortals a release from their reality, while they damned him to wallow in confusion without reprieve.

He stirred his tasteless drink with his middle finger, which he did only because he had seen others do it, and as the liquid spun he licked the wine from his digit. When that no longer amused him he thought about the song Ariana had sung for him. She always knew how to please him.

He knew he was avoiding the truth of what troubled him. On his way to the tavern, while walking through the woods, he had run into the corpse of a man killed by supernatural means. Rancour's temples pounded as he recalled the grotesque body. Claw marks raked down his chest and a creature had feasted upon the legs and stomach.

He would have guessed it was probably a werewulf, but after scanning it he'd found two tiny bite-marks in the jugular. It was now clear that a vampyre was in the hamlet's midst.

Several other murders had already occurred, all bearing the wulf's marks. Until tonight they hadn't disturbed him all that much, but this one had occurred close to his home. The villagers thought it was the act of a mad wulf, and Rancour knew that he had to stop transforming. He had no wish to be caught and falsely accused. He wondered if all the corpses had a hidden vampyre's trademark.

He sighed, glad that the merchant had stayed with Ariana. Should the vampyre strike there, frail as Shay may be, he could at least provide a diversion for Ariana to escape. Rancour wondered how safe his loved one was with Shay, who was only mortal. She'd protected them by hanging wolfsbane on the door and crafting a knife from silver, just as the villagers had done. Had she known it was a vampyre she would have donned a cross and refused to invite *in any stranger who happened by.*

Rancour had once thought those measures enough to protect himself.

He now had to accept, because of his own supernatural powers, that those superstitions were false prejudice. He was, after all, a werewulf and no wolfsbane harmed him. Neither did the full moon make him transform nor had he ever desired to eat a man's flesh. So how then could he believe that a cross or garlic would turn away a vampyre, or even that the beasts could not come out in the daylight? If the vampyre legends were as false as his own, and this one had a taste for man, then these mortal villagers were as good as dead.

His own powers made him feel responsible to end this demon's terror. But by making a life with Ariana had he not chosen a life of peace and forsaken battle? Supernatural or not, was it his duty to stop the carnage?

"I meet you well, friend," a voice said.

Rancour glanced up to see a short, rotund man smiling at him. His heart stopped. The man's wide eyes displayed a very vibrant life-force. Normally that would be a natural and fair trait, but in this person it had come as a shock. This was the same poor gent he had just seen in the woods … murdered by a beast of superstition!

A beast such as himself.

The night suffered from thick darkness and Rancour hadn't taken a lamp on his trek when he had seen the corpse, but he knew he was not mistaken. He could never forget such grey hair, thick as though lightning had struck it. He mustered a smile for courage and replied, "Y-you are met well, but I … I fear solitude is mine companion this night. P-please forgive me impudence."

The short stranger took it upon himself to sit. Rancour's heart raced as though it might leap from his chest and, as though to offer it that escape, his mouth dropped. He sipped at his drink and inquired, "What brings you out this night, goodly Sir?"

"My name is Indigo Anterion...."

"Please, Sir," he looked everywhere but at the man, "forgive me impudence. But ... did I not just see you out in the woods ... quite dead?"

Indigo turned a pale shade of white like no human Rancour had ever seen. He slowly inhaled a long breath of smoky air and sighed, smiling wide.

"'T'was not I, my friend. Obviously I am alive and quite well."

Rancour laughed away his fear. This could not possibly be the same gent he had seen in the woods. He didn't even possess a single scar! Forgetting his foolishness Rancour allowed him to finish his words.

"I am out vampyre hunting."

Rancour checked another laugh. "Per'aps you should consider a drink, instead."

"I would, indeed, care for a glass of milk. Even if it is from a goat." Indigo leaned back in his chair and stared, smiling all the while. He rested his hands on his large belly and asked with a sorrowful tone, "Are you curious why alcohol has no taste?"

"Aye," Rancour replied without thinking, sounding much more eager than he would have liked.

"The alcohol is a toxin. A poison, if you will. Your body ... our bodies, cannot be poisoned."

A look so stern that Rancour found himself fearing what knowledge this fellow might have to impart replaced Indigo's smile. Had he been the man in the woods?

"Our bodies?"

"Yes, Rancour. You are not alone. I, too, am immortal. Although, I am not of your brethren."

"And what 'brethren' might you be?"

"You are of a race that began at the world's inception, and will end at its destruction; I am of a race that began at the world's destruction and will end at its inception. The humans call me a 'Descender', though, to them, as to you, I exist as but a legend."

"What do you take me for, an ignorant fool?"

"Perhaps I should take you for an egoist. Are you so ignorant as to believe that only your race exists outside the mortals? I was born in your future, Rancour, and I will die in what is now your past."

The barmaid came around with more drinks, but this time Rancour declined. She shot him a scornful look, glanced at Indigo who mouthed "milk," and left the two immortals to stare at one another. After some time had passed, Indigo added, "What if I told you that I am the man you found in the woods? What if I told you that, because I move backwards in time, my death has not yet occurred? But once I leave this tavern I will die. But to you, someone who lives forward in time, my death has already come to pass."

"I would ask why such a man would come to me."

"I know the rules of your brethren, my friend. As well, I know your future. I have come so that you might survive the tribulations of being immortal. And, so you might survive another race when they come."

"The vampyres?"

"No. There will be another, Rancour. One far worse than the vampyre."

• • •

It amused Indigo that this wolf concerned himself so much with the vampyre. If only he knew the far worse danger that was hunting him. Indigo sat hunched over the steering wheel of his late model Chevy van as Bruce rummaged in the back with swords, guns and body armour. It amused Indigo that this wolf concerned himself so much with the vampyre. If only he knew the far worse danger that was hunting him. Indigo took out a cigarette and lit up. He breathed in the tobacco and savoured the mint flavour as he watched the sky bleed colours of scarlet and amber. The Northern Lights were a phenomenon that amazed him as much this night as they had the first night he had seen them over a century ago.

"Bruce, we need success tonight," he said in a way that was a commandment and not a suggestion.

Bruce stopped gearing up and answered, "Tonight I vow that I will save hundreds, even if I must sacrifice dozens to do so."

Indigo watched from the rear-view mirror. He had seen the fury locked deep within his partner suddenly erupt without provocation and had made a point not to let the rage land on his shoulders. Indigo slipped his free hand into his open jacket and kept his Glock at the ready.

"I will do you proud this night, father," Bruce answered.

Indigo relaxed his grip from the pistol. A solid diet of steroids and philosophy had given him the perfect warrior, one that would do whatever asked without question. One ruled by the most powerful of motivations: vengeance.

"The man who killed your birth parents is out there, tonight, Bruce. I am beginning to think you don't really want him dead. Is that why you allow him to add more victims to his carnage?"

"I will not allow him to continue to mock me." Bruce sounded angrier now. "Tonight, I will end his carnage and send a message to all unholy beasts! Tonight will be MY VENGEANCE!"

Indigo smiled as he watched Bruce leap from the side door of the van and run off into the night.

Derrick sat near the river that cut through Sunset Park and stared up into the starry night. Behind him trees stood tall as a barrier, shielding him from the road where cops often drove past. Seven of his gang stood about, each one a warrior waiting for a command from their leader. A leader whose focus was on the brilliant Northern Lights.

This was not his last year of high school. And yet it was. He'd been held back twice now and no doubt would be held back again this year. What was the point, anyway? He could go farther north and find work that didn't require a high school education. But first there was one thing he needed to do.

Nathan emerged from the woods, "Kharl left. There were too many cops comin' by to kick his butt, anyway."

Derrick stayed stoic, the sound of the rushing river filling his ears. His one hand he held tight in a fist, the broken one lay over his lap.

"Tomorrow then. Tomorrow we'll do the town a favor..."

"Perhaps," said a man, unknown to any of the boys. "You can do the town a favor tonight."

The man stepped out from the night and stood but a

few feet from Derrick. He was tall, muscular and broad shouldered. Bigger than Arnold Swartzenegger in his prime. A sword was strapped to his back, a gun holstered at his waist and a machete slung across his chest. Derrick did not look at him, did not move; he only smiled and spoke.

"What the fuck you want?"

The giant laughed a deep throaty chuckle. He spread his arms wide and said, "I am your salvation!"

Derrick stood as his gang circled the giant. "My salvation? You think I can't kick your ass?" He stepped forward just as a wind started to stir among the poplar trees. "You think I'm scared just 'cause you come armed?"

"Do you wish to save thousands?"

Nathan rushed the giant from behind but was knocked out cold by one sweep of the stranger's arm. Two others rushed in but were as quickly subdued by a sidekick and punch. The giant wasn't even winded. Before any more of Derrick's gang stepped up the leader shouted, "Enough!"

The giant slowly pulled his sword from its sheath as he held Derrick's glare. Derrick knew he was in trouble, but he wasn't about to show it. He took out his knife and puffed out his chest. No one was going to make a fool out of him!

Then he heard Rellik behind him say, "Derrick, this is not your fight."

Derrick stepped sideways to keep both the giant and Rellik in his view. Both of them had swords at the ready, both were poised to fight. Before anyone could fully process what was going on, the two strangers to this town ran at one another and clashed swords. They fought hard and fast, metal sparking against metal beneath a shower of Northern Lights.

The three of Derrick's gang who hadn't got knocked out picked up the three who had. They rushed to Derrick and grabbed his arm, pulling him from the fray. Derrick freed himself from his buddy's grasp as Rellik took a gash in the side and fell to the grass. Without thinking, Derrick threw his knife as hard as he could, hitting the giant in the shoulder and stopping a blow that would have gone straight through Rellik's chest. And just as he did, just as the giant fell a few steps back and dropped his sword, Rellik shape-shifted into a wolf and bound away into the woods. The giant followed fast behind him.

CHAPTER 10

"Evil, I once thought, was a birthright passed on in the same way as the color of one's eyes. As I grew from an infant to a man I believed that my clan was evil, and, because I was one of them, so must I also be. After all, we fought together, we killed together and we conquered together. What I could not understand, however, was why no one but I saw our bane.

"When I left the Alsandair I feared their lessons would never leave me, and that I would always be tempted into selfishness. What confused me was the virtue left in me by my true blood-line, the Wulfsign, a clan I never even knew.

"Often I contemplate: Is evil an ailment of ignorance, or a genetic disposition from which there is no escape?"

— Wulfsign

lix opened her eyes as a chill breeze enveloped her. She lay on her bed, tucked deep within her blankets, dressed in warm flannel pyjamas. Brisk air crawled into the bed with her, even though the bedroom window was closed. As Alix shrugged off sleep's iron grasp she wondered why she grew suddenly cold. She pulled her comforter tighter around herself, closed her eyes and tried to sleep.

"Look into the orb!" bellowed a raspy voice as the chill air lifted her blankets from her.

Alix woke fully and froze in terror. Where did that voice come from? Was she still asleep? Was this a dream, one so vivid that she felt awake? It had to be, didn't it? Normal people didn't hear voices! *It is a dream,* Alix reassured herself. Alix held her eyes shut, unable to keep her body from shaking. Sitting up, Alix breathed deeply, thinking of how her warm blankets felt when she was deep inside them, and what it was like when she was asleep inside her room. What she was experiencing was only a nightmare, and if she thought hard enough she could easily pull herself from it. Right?

Wrong.

Alix opened her eyes. She was in a tiny, cubicle of a room with no windows or doors. Her mind felt dizzy as if the room had begun to spin, and to keep steady she braced her palms on her bed. But her bed slowly sank into the floor, leaving her sitting upright on a clammy floor. A mist formed in the air around her, the cold water droplets swirling about like stars. As they spun they crashed into one another and they stuck together, until there was only one crystal ball-shaped orb hovering above her lap. Tears welled in her sleepy eyes as she buried them in her palms. *How,* she wondered, *can I stop this nightmare from continuing?*

She held her head high. Her breathing was heavy and her heart raced. A gnarled arm burst from the floor beside her and grabbed the orb. Alix screamed and moved away from it, but the wall came up against her and pushed her back to the orb. Alix bit her lip and peered inside.

A girl her age, wearing tight spandex that looked as though it had been painted onto her thin legs, stared at the stars while picking flowers by the road. She carried a short red leather jacket adorned with long tassels, though Alix could see by her puffy breaths that the air was cold.

When Alix glimpsed the girl's face she whispered, "Betty," and her eyes swelled with tears.

"Look into the orb," the cold, raspy voice demanded. She chose to obey rather than risk its unknown wrath.

Alix caressed the cold glass and watched her best-friend meet a stranger blocked from recognition by dark shadows. He and Betty spoke with one another as though they were acquaintances, and she reacted as her flirtatious self. He took her hand into his and they walked off the trail into some bushes. He kissed her, and she grabbed the back of his neck and kissed him. As their lust created a fire strong enough to warm them, their coats fell to the ground.

The stranger stopped kissing Betty and lifted his face up-ward as if to look directly at Alix. Red eyes burned through the mist, but the haze still obscured his face. Alix wondered who he might be.

But before she could scream a warning, fog encased the picture and all she heard was a cry of terror.

Alix pushed the orb away, unable to bring herself to look back into it. She whispered over and over: "This is only a dream," but even when she pinched herself she could not wake.

A light grew and shrank from the orb, as if it beckoned her to see what had happened. She didn't know what to do and relaxed only when she rubbed the bottom of her nose. She had decided to give in when she heard the faint ring of a telephone.

Closing her eyes tight, she concentrated with all her strength on the telephone. As the ring grew louder, Alix feared the ball would call to her, but as the darkness fell upon her as if to crush her she....

Woke up.

Terrified at how real the vision of Betty's demise had been.

Alix shook off the terrible nightmare and realized that her phone really had been ringing. She reached over the side of the bed to where she had left it earlier that evening, and took a moment to glance at the clock. 3:17 am.

"Hello?"

"Alexandria?" her best-friend's mother said on the other end. "May I speak with my daughter?"

"Ms. Black?" Alix asked more to stall time than because she didn't know who it was.

"Yes, Alix. Is Betty there?"

"No, we were all at Icy Shakes, but we didn't leave together. I think she walked away with Simon."

"Okay," Ms. Black said, fear strong in her short response.

Alix said good-bye and hung up the phone. She considered for a moment calling Simon or Kharl, but that would mean believing that her dream was real. Climbing out of bed she walked to her Pooh Bear and cuddled into its lap, where she spent the rest of this restless night.

CHAPTER 11

lix stared past her timetable that hung inside her locker. She had already taken out her Math and Lit texts, but at least ten minutes remained before first period and she wanted to wait for Betty.

"Hey," a voice said from behind. Alix spun and saw it was Kharl. He didn't look at her and stood straight with a rigid jaw. When he spoke he did so matter-of-factly, and it made Alix nervous. "Have you seen Betty?"

"Why?" Alix closed her locker door and rubbed the bottom of her nose. "You know, I wasn't even aware we were still speaking."

"You know what? I was drunk last night. That's my excuse for acting like a jerk, so what's yours?"

Alix could hear Betty tell her to just let things be and give in to Kharl. She wanted to go to the dance, to be asked by the most popular guy in school, and to have just one normal year of high school.

"Sorry," she whispered just loud enough for him to hear.

"Y'know, Betty's mom phoned my house last night. Crazy woman phoned Simon's, too. Betty never came home."

"She phoned me, too," Alix started to say but stopped. Was her dream real? Did she watch Betty die? "I have to go. I have Lit class." Alix turned to walk away, but bumped into Simon.

"Hey, watch it! Either of you guys seen Betty?"

Both Alix and Kharl shook their heads.

Simon muttered, "There's a rumor there was another wolf attack last night."

Alix felt tears well in her eyes and stormed away.

Alix knew her nightmare was real. She'd seen what had really happened. She wanted to talk to Fred, to throw her arms around him and cry, but she couldn't. She could never tell him because of his emotional attachment to Betty. Even though she needed to open her heart as she never had before, she'd have to go through this alone.

"Hey, Alix, wait up!" It was Simon.

She stopped, feeling a tear escape her eye.

"Have you heard from Betty?"

"No. Really, I haven't."

"Well, if you do, tell her we need to talk. She stormed out after I stopped her from fighting you. This is kind of your fault, you know."

Alix shook her head and held tears at bay. Slowly turning from Simon she walked the hallway, feeling for the first time how long and empty it truly was.

Then from behind she heard: "Blondie!"

Alix spun and saw Kim. "Hey."

"Wow. You aren't afraid of me anymore. I must be losing it."

"Look, I'm not in the mood, okay?" Alix wiped her eyes, hoping she wouldn't start crying now. Not in front of Kim.

"Hey, none of my business. I got a way for you to make things up to me."

"What's that?"

"My brother wants Kharl to meet him by the dumpster after school."

"Another fight?"

"Why would you say that? Because we're Indian?"

"No. I don't know why I said it."

"Look, just do it or don't. We'll be there."

Ten minutes after the noon bell, Alix was standing outside the cafeteria. She didn't know if she could face everyone gossiping about Betty. Deciding she couldn't, she turned away. Shay was standing in the hall not far off, and he approached until he loomed over her with a wide smile. Alix took it as a welcome escape from her friends.

"And what, pray tell, is troubling your dear heart?" he asked in his sweet tenor voice.

There was that deviant twist in his smile again. He was handsome, and just the kind of guy Betty went after. Tears swelled in Alix's eyes.

"N-nothing." Alix turned away and tried to keep her voice from shaking.

Shay brushed his index finger beneath her chin and brought her face back to his. There was something sensual about the action. His eyes grew wide, and his pupils dilated. Alix was drawn into them, feeling her pain subside as a cloud-like consciousness entered her heart.

His voice relaxed her, but she could not make out the words. It was like a hand reaching into her soul and stroking her pain away. It seemed as if the hand were closing around a piece of her soul, but before she realized that it intended to take that piece from her it was too late. As the hand pulled away, everything that had seemed so important became a dream. When the cloud lifted and Alix regained her senses, she thought about her friend's death no more.

"I–I'm sorry, Shay ... I must have been daydreaming." She blinked as though she had, indeed, just woken from a deep slumber. "Were you saying something?"

Shay chuckled.

• • •

Rellik sighed again and wondered where to search next. He had started looking for Fred long before the noon bell and had hoped to have found him by now. Peering into the library he finally saw the teen he sought inside studying. He turned away, reasoning that since Fred was obviously busy he shouldn't disturb him. But he turned back; he had to stay true to his task. There were, after all, no other options.

Fred had his long nose tucked neatly between the pages of the play Hamlet. He jerked when Rellik slammed a chair down from across the small table, but never lifted his head from the depth of his book. He held it as a shield between them.

Rellik sat but said nothing. He stared, his large brow low and tight. He tilted his head slightly forward. He listened to Fred's heart race as he pulled the book down. The teen's eyes widened.

Rellik sighed, the sudden exhaust of air sounding like a low growl ... a low, menacing growl. Fred opened his mouth as if to speak, but nothing came out. He gripped his book tighter as drool seeped from his mouth.

That's disgusting, Rellik thought. He relaxed and said

aloud, trying to sound kindly, "I need your aid," but his teeth remained locked in a snarl.

"Sure," Fred said, his voice breaking at soprano level and making a startling bird-like chirp.

Rellik had the floor and wondered what he should say. He wanted so much to tell this teen, to tell anyone for that matter, everything about who he was. But what if Fred thought of him as a creature and shunned him? He wanted so much to believe there was just one person in this world who could look past the myths and see him for who he was.

And not for what they thought him to be.

Rancour, lying peacefully in the darkness, looked beside him where Ariana lay sound asleep. He wondered how much longer he could keep his secret of immortality from her, and what she would do once she learned the truth. Indigo's clandestine lessons of the Wulfsign and the religion that bound them were going well. Every day Rancour learned more about living with the knowledge that he would never meet death. But tonight, when he had thought about what Ariana might do when she saw him transform, for someday she would mistakenly see it happen, he'd lost the ability to sleep. He knew she would leave him because of her mortal fear of the unknown, and sighing sadly, he could not blame her. His only hope was to stop the vampyre before she found out, so he could stop being the wulf. That way he could live with her for her entire mortal life without her ever seeing him in his canine form.

His teacher never discussed how to kill other immortals, and Rancour wondered what truth, if any, lay in the myths surrounding the vampyres. He rolled onto his side and stroked Ariana's long hair. He checked a laugh as he thought about Indigo's warning that he relied too much on physical brute strength and didn't balance it enough with intellect. *How Kendil would have begged to differ.* For days his tutor had pressured him to learn to write a "journal", and at first, Rancour had scoffed at such foolishness. In the end he agreed to learn on the condition that Indigo never pressure him again about the value of literacy. But philosophy, the discussion of values and morals, now that was a thing Rancour loved.

"'Tis not our powers that cause mortals to fear us," his tutor had told him earlier that day, "for does the chameleon not imitate its surroundings? Does the bird not fly? And yet mortals respect their power as beauty."

"Then what do they fear?" Rancour had asked, not looking away from the journal entry he had begun to write.

"Intellect, Rancour. They fear a beast that is unlike them, yet every bit as intelligent."

"But if it were not for our powers we could 'ide as a mortal." Rancour liked to challenge him. It gave him special pleasure whenever he stumped his tutor.

"But there are those of us who are evil. Some who think that immortality gives them the right to be gods. You must never abuse your powers."

"The vampyre is like that! Tell me 'ow to fight 'im."

"Learn about your own kind. Learn about the Wulfsign, and the code you must follow. With power comes responsibility."

"Why is it you 'ave no powers? You are immortal. Why do mortals fear your kind?"

"I know how I die. And, at one time, I thought myself divine enough to avenge it."

"Do you know when you die? Do you know 'ow I die?"

"We will speak no more. Write, Rancour. Write your thoughts

in your journal. You have more knowledge than you give yourself credit for."

The solemn look that befell his tutor brought Rancour back to where he lay in his bed beside Ariana. She smiled in her sleep, and just knowing how much she loved him brightened his dark thoughts. If she learned of his difference she would have questions, inquiries for which he had no answers. But so long as the murders resumed in the hamlet he could not forsake his responsibility to become the werewulf. Only as the wulf did his hearing, night vision, and perception heighten enough to win an advantage over the vampyre. Whoever he might be.

He prayed Ariana would understand when she learned of his difference. But it was much to expect when he couldn't accept it himself. At least he had Indigo to teach him what it was to be immortal.

"Fred," Rellik whispered, letting his emotions guide his words for the first time in centuries, "tell me what it is to feel human again."

• • •

Some time later Rellik found Alexandria in the hallway just outside the cafeteria ... with Shay. Her one hand rested on his chest, and the other rubbed his arm whenever he cracked a joke. Rellik wondered how Shay could dupe everyone into believing his act, but as his adversary slipped his arm playfully around Alexandria's shoulders and tickled her nose, he wondered no more. It was that damn perfected charm. Shay had a natural gift for knowing what to wear and what to say. Hell, even his gentlemanly grooming made him appear trustworthy.

Rellik looked at himself. His entire wardrobe consisted of sweats and muscle shirts. He wondered why. *Comfort*, he told himself. But at least he could have shaved the two-day stubble from his square jaw or cut his long hair to appear respectable. He turned from his task, but before walking away he took one last look at Shay and Alexandria.

No! Rellik thought, stopping in his tracks as though he had come against a spiritual wall. *There is still Ariana's soul in her. Do not let her get away!* Taking a deep breath he marched to her with his fists clenched by his side.

"Good day, Rellik!" Shay said charmingly as he took his arm away from around Alexandria. "I was just departing." Then he looked at her and said, "I shall miss you so, my sweet."

The vamp's tone rang confidently and his mockery sounded all too familiar. Rellik wondered what that devil was up to. Even after Shay had walked away, and not before he'd kissed Alexandria's hand, he still kept within earshot of them.

Alix relaxed as though she had come off a drug, and when the numbness left she had a sensation that she'd forgotten something important. But she hadn't a clue what that something might be, and it did not matter right now. Rellik had come to speak with her, though he only stared at her with sad eyes. She opened her mouth to say something but stopped herself.

Not this time, she decided. She only offered the leather jacket he had surrendered to her the previous night.

"Hello, Alexandria. I pray I am well met ... I mean, uhm, nice day," he stumbled, avoiding her eyes.

"It is a nice day, Rellik. And a good thing, too. I have class right away." She wondered why she wished to keep this conversation short.

"My apologies for delaying you. Perchance we can speak later."

"Yeah, maybe." Alix turned to walk away.

"The dance?" he suddenly asked, the question sounding harsh and forced out.

A long pause followed his question, and as Alix turned back to him she answered, "What about it? Are you going?"

Rellik met her gaze, scanned the room and breathed hard. Rather abruptly he said, "Only if you should accompany me."

"To the dance?" In a quiet voice she said, "I've already been asked by Shay."

Rellik's face burned and his muscles had begun to shake. In a flash he whipped on his sunglasses and growled:

"Then perchance you might save me a waltz." He sighed and, taking his jacket, he left.

Alix felt as though a truck had hit her. *What the heck was that all about?* she wondered, wishing to say much more to him. If only she knew what. At first the outsider appeared to have interest in nothing but solitude, but now he did something that took heart. Perhaps all he needed was more time?

But what would I give him more time for? she thought.

Rellik stormed past Shay, but not before glaring into his eyes and replying telepathically, "You haven't won yet."

The vamp glared back but Rellik had already broken

the mind-bond and stormed toward Dead Man's Alcove. He sensed not only Shay's presence close behind, but also his wish to settle their last score.

After all, they had yet to gamble for the ultimate prize.

Once inside the alcove Shay grabbed Rellik's left shoulder from behind. The Wulfsign pivoted, brought his left arm down on the vamp's elbow joint and, using his opponent's obvious "advantage" of leverage against him, he twisted the arm and pinned him against the lockers. Rellik smiled.

Shay said, "Your training has served you well, Wulfsign. But I have not challenged you."

"Matter of interpretation. Like the challenge you gave me a thousand years ago," Rellik growled as he cautiously released him.

"My friend, from what I recall, you were the challenger. Therefore, according to your philosophy, I had every right to kill you ... be thankful I did not."

"I know the rules. I also know that vampires don't have to abide by them." Rellik glared at his enemy, wishing he'd had this knowledge a millennium before.

Wishing he had known when Shay was setting him up for his games....

Rain poured as if to wipe evil from the face of the Earth, but neither Rancour nor Shay paid it any heed. There was hope in the rainbow's shadow far in the horizon, and the field had to be worked. Rancour wiped his brow, stopped and looked at the merchant who sat beneath a parasol upon a patch of grass.

"Why are you not working?" Rancour spat.

"Because I am thinking. Do you never feel the need to set aside meaningless tasks to contemplate important matters?"

"Meaningless tasks? If we do not tend the field, we shall not grow anything. If we grow nothing, we cannot pay our taxes. If we do not pay our taxes, we shall lose the land."

"Are you telling me that you work the land to pay taxes, so that you can keep working the land? That seems quite stupid and meaningless."

"What is so stupid and meaningless about it?"

"If you do not have the land, you would not owe any taxes. Therefore, if you lost the land all you would really lose is the need to pay tax. There is more to life than taxes, Wulfsign."

"Why do you call me that?"

"What?"

"Wulfsign! Why do you not call me by my given name?"

"I thought I was showing you respect by calling you by your clan's name."

"I do not appreciate it. What I would appreciate is you getting on with your duties. Fetch me some water."

"Fetch some water?" Shay fell into a bow. "T'would be my honor; I am your servant."

"Why do you say it like that?"

"Say it like what? Master, just snap your fingers and I shall obey."

"You are getting on me nerves."

"And you shall do what about this?"

"I will forgive you this impudence. But should it continue, I shall send you on your way."

"The hospitality is not yours to offer, nor is it yours to take away."

"The 'ome may be Ariana's, but 'er 'eart is mine. Should I ask, she would send you on your way."

The merchant circled Rancour as he taunted, "Such a pity that a man of your stature would need a woman to cower behind. She will make good children, perhaps it is mine she should bear. That way her blood-line will have real men. Men who know when a challenge is in order."

"Do not test me! Do you think you can best me? I am Rancour the Wulfsign, o' the clan Alsandair!"

"You are a drifter wandering without a clan. You, my friend, are less than nothing."

Rancour ran at the merchant and grabbed his tunic. Throwing Shay to the ground the Wulfsign spit upon him.

"Is that a challenge?" the merchant asked.

"Aye it is. Per'aps if I show you what it means to fight an Alsandair, you will know what it means to respect one!"

Rancour wondered why Shay stood before him with a smile from ear to ear. He had, after all, just walked into his death. Rancour felt like a wooden soldier in a child's game ... and he swore he heard Ansgar's laugh in the drops of rain that fell upon him.

"Do you really believe you are more learned than I, you pitiful beast?" Shay said, mimicking words from an ancient past.

They stopped circling and stood as if caught in suspended animation.

"What do you suggest, Shay?" Rellik growled, focusing on his combination.

Shay turned to his own locker and also fiddled with his bolt. Time neared one in the afternoon, and, as the lethargic students turned into moving traffic in the halls, the vamp made sure to keep his back to Rellik. When the lock clicked he asked, while opening the door and gathering his books, "You still drive that Mopar-shit of yours?"

Rellik breathed deeply to cool his temper. He hated it when Shay referred to his 'Cuda like that.

"Yes I do still drive my 'Mopar-shit'. You still drive that 'rare import' of yours?"

"Rare import." Shay swayed back in a hefty laugh. "I do believe my five litre Mustang could stomp your little fish. Unlike you, I trade antiques for modern fare."

Rellik liked the way this conversation was headed. It was simple logic he could outrun Shay's Mustang, and this duel's prize could be but one thing. Flexing his bulk to its fullest definition he replied, "Is that a challenge?"

Shay smiled and said, "Yes it is. My, you have matured these past thousand years."

"What are the stakes?"

The bell rang, signalling the students to get to class. The two immortals ignored the resounding buzz as each stared into the other's soul, both recalling a time when they had struck a similar deal.

"The loser leaves town ... alone," Shay said, walking to the alcove's entrance. Turning back he added, "This time there will be none of your tricks."

Rellik smiled, calling, "You did not like my interpretation of leaving town last time?"

But the vamp had already gone.

• • •

"Why do you suppose Alix told us to meet her here?" Simon asked, throwing the pop can he'd just emptied beside the dumpster.

"Better be to apologize for avoiding me all day," Kharl answered.

"So why'd she ask me to come?"

"She and Betty are probably playing some stupid joke on us. You know girls."

"Well, there she is, and it isn't Betty she's with."

"What the hell?"

Alix, Kim, Derrick and six native males advanced toward them. The girls stopped on Kharl's left as the rest approached on the right. Derrick held something in his hands.

"It's time to end this," the native youth said.

"I've been set up?"

"Yes, but not for what you think," Derrick stuck out his hand, "I want to make peace."

"Why? You punk chicken shit admitting I can kick yer ass?"

"I'm saying it doesn't matter. Hatred is making us weak, not strong."

"Strong? You want strong?" The jock lashed out and slugged Derrick across the cheek. Pointing at Alix he said, "You and me have got some serious talking to do."

As Derrick hit the ground his friends stepped forward. Raising his hands to stop them he yelled, "No! Smoke my grandfather's pipe. It's time to end this!"

Kharl shook his head. "Let's not. C'mon, get up and get your ass kicked."

Derrick stood and looked briefly at his gang. They waited to see what he would do. Facing Kharl he walked up to the jock and said, "Can't you see there's something big going on in Minitaw? We should be banding together to stop it!"

Kharl smiled, "That's what I thought." He shoved Derrick away and pointed to Alix. "You coming?"

She looked at Kim and shrugged. "I'll see you later."

"No. We'll leave." Derrick signalled his friends to follow.

Kharl waited for them to vacate before saying to Alix, "What was that?"

"What?"

"You know what. Pull that again and you can get another date for Friday."

"I already have. Shay asked me."

Kharl closed his eyes and breathed hard. "I'm trying not to get real mad here."

"You don't own me!" Alix yelled and stormed away.

Kharl looked at Simon, who shrugged and said, "Maybe there is something big going on in Minitaw."

CHAPTER 12

"When mortals learned that only a blow through
our heart can end the life of an immortal, they
abominated that knowledge by instilling an absurd
legend around it. To kill us they use wooden stakes,
herbs or crosses. Whatever the tool, the ignorance
always amazes me.
"Whenever I try to understand those who kill my
kind, and those of my kind who kill them, I do so
without success. Mostly, I wonder who is more evil:
those who kill for the hunt, or those who kill out
of prejudice."

                                        —Wulfsign

Rellik drove his 'Cuda from its hiding place and parked it on the street in front of Alix's home. In a matter of an hour he'd adjusted the timing, put in new plugs, cleaned and adjusted the carburetor, and filled the tank with a high octane fuel. As he stood before his prized possession on the lonely street he prepared for the last thing he had left to do: clean and polish the immaculate body.

He wanted his "little fish" to look good when it beat Shay.

"Hi, Rellik. What're you up to?" Fred said from behind, startling the outsider. He walked to the soapy bucket, grabbed a sponge and started cleaning the dust from the car's hood.

Rellik sighed. "I'm washing the 'Cuda. If you wish to aid me, I'll take you for a ride."

His guard returned in full force, but a yearning to accept friendship battled it. If he was to win Alexandria's heart and live out a normal mortal existence he needed to accept people. Besides, Fred pleased him, almost as much as Indigo had. He half-smiled, picked up some polish-soaked paper towels and chucked one to Fred before starting on one of the wheels.

"I hear you and Shay are racing. It isn't for ownership of the car, I hope," Fred said.

"Not for pinks." Rellik frowned. "The winner has sole rights to stay in town."

Fred stopped cleaning and grimaced. His brow dropped, his eyes narrowed and he rubbed his chin.

"You're going to race for the right to stay in town? How barbaric. What is it between you two that only one of you can stay in town?"

Rellik had long since finished polishing the mag to a mirror finish, but he continued scrubbing to avoid Fred's judgment. Without looking at his new friend he asked, "Have you ever known someone who is truly evil?"

Fred's face drew taut and color flushed into his cheeks. He tapped his fingers on the hood where he had been cleaning, and hoping Rellik wouldn't notice the new fingerprints.

"No. I have always found good in everyone. I believe it's okay to hate an individual's actions, but never the individual."

Rellik walked around him to the other wheel, kneeled, but did not polish. He faced Fred, stared into his eyes, and, from the scent of perspiration in the air, acknowledged his friend's uncertainty toward this conversation.

"What if you knew someone so vile that there was no goodness in him?" He stood, keeping his gaze locked on Fred's. "What if you found a person who took all ambiguity out of defining what good and evil is?"

He took the sponge from Fred's hand, turned his back on him, and dipped it into the soapy bucket. Rellik lifted it and as he squeezed out the excess water he watched the cool liquid run down the length of his arm. Then he said, "And what if you were helpless to stop it?"

"Y-you're going to win, right?"

Rellik wondered if Fred was more afraid of him losing and leaving or winning and staying. He sighed, and put the wet sponge into his friend's hand. Gently, he started him polishing the car's hood in a small, circular motion.

"Keep cleaning."

"But good versus evil ... good always wins, right?"

Rellik picked up a bottle of window-cleaner and another rag. He walked to the back of the 'Cuda, sprayed it onto the mirrored rear-view glass and stared at his broken reflection. As he rubbed it clean he....

...burst through the cabin door, slammed it shut and threw the brace. His dark complexion had turned a pale hue that Ariana had never seen before and his hands shook. He ran to her, grabbed her roughly and pulled her to the ground. As each met the other's gaze they rose to their knees, and when Rancour tried to speak he found that his voice failed.

"What kind of devil has gotten into you?" Ariana asked, never having seen her love quite so fearful. He was strong-willed and sure of himself by nature.

"'e's a demon, Ariana!" Rancour finally said, his eyes darting about the room to ensure he had secured all entrances. "'e turned to mist right in me grasp!"

"Of whom do you speak? You frighten me!" Her voice shook, and though she had tried holding tears at bay they gushed down her reddened cheeks.

Rancour stared into her wet eyes and sensed her terror and put aside his own. He had made a bargain with the Devil and would have to fulfill it, but his first duty was still to her. He was ashamed for agreeing to the stakes and, as well, that his honor bound him to comply.

But did honor take precedence over love?

"My apologies, Ariana. I speak of Shay, for a merchant 'e is not. Lest 'e be one o' souls and mine be his next purchase. Forgive me, I knew not with what I bargained. I must fight 'im, or be banished from an 'ome I 'ave come to love." His voice resounded with shame, but he decided that shame was by far a better emotion to show than fear.

The cabin's floor became their place of safety as Ariana wrapped her arms tightly around her love's neck. She prayed he would never leave, but knew the stubborn strength that bound him to his honor, a trait with which she had fallen in love. He had to return to meet Shay on the field of battle, and as she released her tight grip from him she did so only enough to meet his eyes. She dared not release him fully.

"You can fare better than he, can you not?"

Rellik stared deeply into the mirrored glass. He laughed at the strange camaraderie he had found with the car, and realized that, after having spent so long without human contact, he had forgotten what it was to truly rely on a friend.

Now he had come full circle, but this time to wonder why the vamp would choose a duel that took away his advantage.

"This has nothing to do with good or evil," Rellik said, just now understanding the vamp's insidious plan. "This battle has to do with my car faring better than his!"

Alix watched as Rellik and Fred worked on the 'Cuda. She debated for a moment if she should go outside and join them, or if she should just leave them alone to bond. Then she turned from the living-room window and walked out the back door.

Alix was first overcome by the odor of oil, second by the smell of spray-paint. She looked over to where Sam sat hunched on a lawn chair. He buried his face in his palms.

As Alix moved toward him she said, "Hey, Sam."

He stood and spun around, a smile forced over his sad expression. He looked so old as he said, "I hadn't realized how much stuff I'd let pile up. The only thing that we'll need to call someone for is the garage door. I think it needs a new opener." He walked up to his daughter and put his hands on her shoulders. He added, "Just look at that barbeque! I've covered all the rust spots. No more embarrassment when you have your backyard parties!"

Alix brushed his hands off her shoulders and stared at him. Tears welled in her wide eyes and her hands shook. Though it was like she breathed under water she managed to say, "Stop it."

"What?" Sam asked with sadness evident in his tone.

"Stop pretending that nothing's wrong. Stop pretending that you don't crave booze. Stop pretending that you can change things with WD40 and some paint!" She stared at him and whispered, "Stop pretending that you don't hurt."

Alix looked at his feet; he looked just over her shoulder. Clouds slowly rolled back in, and the sun disappeared. A breeze rose and pushed away the heat. Sam sighed.

"Alix, I don't know what to do." And suddenly tears fell from his eyes. When he reached to wipe them Alix grabbed his wrists and held them fast.

"Cry, Sam. Let yourself cry!" she said and held him. At first he did not respond, but as the rain came down upon the roof he wrapped his arms around her and wept. In his sobs he said, "I am so sorry, honey."

Alix rested her head on his chest. She thought about her mom, of how sad she always seemed whenever Sam was "too tired" to help out around the house. Would she be proud of him now, or would she have considered this "too little, too late"?

"Honey," Sam whispered, "I need to finish up here. Why don't you go inside and start dinner?"

"Okay," Alix said. She walked from him to a cushioned patio chair, with a sweater draped over it. As she put on the sweater there was a loud roar that shattered the peace. As the ground rumbled beneath her, Alix walked around the house to the front.

Rellik was staring at his car with his brow furrowed. His intense glare told her that something very important rode on his vehicle's performance, and she wondered what. She knew only what everyone else in school did: that Rellik and Shay were to meet at Devil's Highway to drag their cars down the one-mile strip.

Rellik, standing over the engine, held up his hand and Fred pressed on the gas pedal. The outsider brushed his hand through his hair, leaving a trail of grease over his brow. The car door creaked open and Fred wandered over to him, also staring at the engine. He imitated the gesture with his hand, but no grease stained him.

"Do you think this'll be enough?" Fred asked.

"Shay will not be the victor of this duel. Of that I am certain." Rellik never met him eye to eye and seemed almost as if he was trying to avoid visual contact.

"Hi, guys." Alix startled them both. "What're you up to?"

Rellik slammed the hood shut and flinched when it echoed. He sighed and growled, "We have just finished readying the 'Cuda for its race tonight."

"So, I'm too late to help?"

"I am about to drive Fred home. You may accompany us if it pleases you." He never looked at her and clenched his muscles tight.

"I'd like that," she said, smiling.

The three of them piled into the 'Cuda and sped off. The incredible power roared all around her, and indeed, it impressed her that its raw power handled so coolly beneath Rellik's fingertips. But it was no different than other muscle cars, and she knew, with all their tinkering, they must have done something to it. Visually, yet discretely, she searched about the interior. She had the benefit of some knowledge from her autoshop class, but try as she might to find anything odd, all she could see was an average dash. Nothing unusual, except....

Then she noticed it.

It was only a tiny something, hardly anything at all. In fact, unless someone was as curious as she was, they would probably have overlooked it. A toggle switch crudely drilled into the dash beside the temperature gauge, now in the "off" position, had a thin red wire leading from it to the carpet on the floor. Where that wire went she had no clue. Another wire, a black one, led from the back of the toggle switch onto a shiny bolt screwed tightly into the dash, cracking the paint.

The car stopped and Fred climbed out. Sticking his head

inside, he said, "Thanks for letting me help. Hope we can get together again."

"I'll pick you up for the race." There was a pause, and after a sigh, he added, "It would be nice to have someone on my side."

"I'll be ready! See ya then!" He waited to help Alix get out, and when he faced her he whispered, "You were right to keep trying for his friendship. He's a good guy."

"So are you," she said and hugged him. Alix watched him walk up to his door, rubbed her nose and got back into the 'Cuda.

Alix wanted to talk, but more so she wanted Rellik to begin the conversation. Yet she said, "I'm sorry about saying no to the dance." Alix wondered why she was never true to her resolutions when it came to this outsider. But what made her even more curious was why she felt so inclined to say yes to the dance. She added, "Kharl asked me after you did. He was pretty mad."

"Then he is a fool to think you should wait on him. Although I, too, thought it strange you would accompany Shay."

"I'm not even sure why I said yes. It was weird, like…"

"…like you were lost in a dream?" he said softly.

"Yes. That's exactly how I felt."

"Perhaps you were overtaken by his charm."

Alix laughed, and suddenly felt completely at ease as she watched him drive. His one hand gripped the small steering wheel while the other rested gently on the stick. She reached out, uncertain as to why, and placed her hand over his on the gear-shifter. His grip tightened and she sensed his body tense, but this time she did not back away. He sighed and relaxed, reaching one of his fingers to interlock with hers. They shifted the powerful car together, as one.

He steered with his elbow, and reaching into his jacket, he took out his sunglasses. As he slapped them over his eyes Alix thought she saw a tear leave one.

"I would rather go to the dance with you."

"Why?" Rellik's voice, losing its darkness, shimmered with sadness. "We do not even know one another."

"Maybe we can change that."

"I would relish that very much."

"For awhile, I was under the impression you didn't want to be friends."

"I did not mean to seem imprudent but I have felt a little out of place here."

The way he'd said "here" made her wonder if he meant the town, or the world itself. She thought about "the girl" in her story and a name flashed through her mind, but it left too quickly for her memory to grasp it.

"I'm glad we're friends now," she said, and as he pulled up snugly against the curb outside her home, she added, "And I think you have twice Shay's charm."

Alix climbed out and glanced back. Rellik watched after her, stunned. Before she disappeared into her house she turned back and saw him gaze at the sky with an expression as if he were praying for the whole world to be his own.

CHAPTER 13

"When a human shares love with a Wulfsign, she
will be reborn one millennium from her first birth.
Should that love be rekindled, it is said that both
mortal and immortal shall grow old and die together.
Both shall join the other's soul in Heaven.
"Many of my brethren opt to live forever rather
than grow old with love. But I am not among
them. I am among those who have loved so deeply
that I would relinquish forever. I am among those
who believe there is more to life than always
seeing tomorrow.
"I am among those who wish to see Heaven."

—Wulfsign

F illmore High's students began to gather around the obsolete strip known as "Devil's Highway". For the past fifty years teens had used it for drag races, which was their means of settling disputes. Most often one driver would lose control and crash, thus giving this strip of pavement its nefarious title.

A red Five-Litre Mustang was first to pull up against the white chalk-line. When the driver flipped a switch on his dash its black top retreated into the back, and as it disappeared, so also did all traces of sun. He looked up into the starry sky as the angels began their colourful dance, and turned his impish grin on a girl who was all alone. He rolled his head back in laughter.

Alix stood without the comfort of friends. They were there, but they stood on the strip's opposite side from her, waiting to cheer Shay to victory as if his triumph would be their own. Kharl had his arm around another girl, one he'd dated last year, someone he'd said meant nothing to him. Alix caught him as he looked over at her, and she diverted his angry gaze.

"Hey, Alix," called a voice from behind.

"Hi," she said, turning to see Kim, Derrick and their friends.

"Where's the Barbie pack?" Kim asked.

Alix looked back at the highway. "Can we not do this?"

Kim walked to stand beside Alix. There was a silence between them until the native girl said, "To think I've spent my entire high school life wanting to be on your side of the highway and now you're on mine."

"You wanted to be our friend? Really?"

"Don't flatter yourself. You'd have to be a whole lot less blonde before we could be friends."

"I'm a whole lot less blonde now."

"Any news on Betty? Rumor is she's disappeared."

"Who?" Again Alix felt the vice on her mind turn a full crank.

Kim laughed. "You're joking, right?"

"No. Who's Betty?"

A loud rumble, as though a chained dragon were waiting escape, stole the girls' attention. Falling silent, they saw Rellik arrive. As he pulled up beside the Five-Litre the two drivers glared at one another briefly. Shay smiled. Rellik hid his emotions behind dark sunglasses. Both revved their engines to show they'd be first to reach the one-mile marker. Fred climbed out of the 'Cuda and looked at Alix who winked at him.

"I wonder if it bothers him," she whispered.

"What?"

"Huh? Oh, sorry. I was talking to myself. I just wondered if it bothered Rellik that so many people want him to lose."

"Are you kidding? Check out the way he's staring at you."

"Don't be ridiculous."

Alix glanced at Rellik. Kim was right. He was looking at her. She wondered why, and watched Fred walk to the chalk-line.

He held a fluorescent-green cloth high above his head and stood between the two cars. The tension intensified like a thunderstorm, and, when the cool wind died, he dropped the cloth. He braced himself as the two vehicles sped by. The immense crowd followed, leaving only Alix, Kim and Fred behind.

"Are you coming?" Kim shouted.

Alix turned and saw Fred sauntering toward her. She shook her head.

"Okay, I'll see you later," Kim said, running to catch the crowd.

Alix wondered why, after all the time he had spent helping Rellik, Fred would lag behind. Did he worry that Shay had spent an equal amount of time fixing up his Mustang? What was so important about winning this race, anyway?

Even more curious was how he had become such good friends with Rellik in such a short time. She filled her lungs with the cool night air as she waited for him to catch up, pausing only to take in the breathtaking sight of the Northern Lights.

Rellik thanked Fate for this second chance to beat Shay, but he also prayed that Destiny's intent was not to mock him. He swore that, over the pounding feet from the stampeding crowd, he could hear Lucifer laugh. He wondered what he would do should he lose this fight.

Rancour had fought hard, but when the battle was finished it was he who lay helpless on the ground. He suffered from a brutal beating, and was now the one in the merchant's debt. They had already agreed to the stakes for the battle, though he could not see what chance he had to win. Every time he'd tried to clout or grapple Shay would turn himself to fog. And those teeth! They were the Devil's own.

Could he leave Ariana with such a demon?

But what was he, if not a demon, too? No blow outside his heart would end his life and more than once he had shape-shifted into the wulf. So what difference did he possess to make him unlike the vampyre?

Rellik listened to Shay shift gears as they neared the finish line. The Mustang still had one left to go, but Rellik had already shifted into his highest gear. He wondered when Shay would shift again, but more so he wondered what that vamp had done to modify his car.

Then, after he heard the 'stang shift, the two immortals met each other's gaze and Shay broke ahead by two full car-lengths. Rellik looked at his unused toggle-switch and hoped his tinkering had been enough. He flicked it. Nothing happened. Then, in a sudden burst of flames, the dragon broke free from its chains, tore the highway with streaks of fire from the exhaust pipes, and roared to win by three full car lengths. As it did, it mocked the Devil by spitting dust into the air.

Rellik screeched to a halt, nearly flipped his 'Cuda, and threw open the door. He stepped out and stretched his arms wide, every muscle on them taut. He smiled, glad that his jaw was tight this time for winning and not losing. The metallic-red Five Litre Mustang sped by, and as it disappeared against the horizon, Rellik watched after it. He yelled victory so loud that the earth shuddered.

Suddenly he felt a presence in his mind. He opened his eyes, concentrated and knew Indigo was near. Indigo always came when it was most inopportune.

Rellik looked upon the Northern Lights, wishing he could have waited for Fred to share his victory. But he had to hide his 'Cuda and hope that Shay led Indigo away. When he looked from the heavens to the Earth below he saw the mad rush of students nearing him and climbed back into his car. He cared nothing for their respect. All that mattered was that he had mocked his enemy. The prize was his, and not the vamp's.

CHAPTER 14

Rellik wondered what he was to do now that he had won. He walked through the iron gate, past the gazebo, and stood beneath his loft. He glanced at Alexandria's window, comforted that it was dark. A sigh escaped him that was carried away by a howling gust, yet was not loud enough to mask another creak from the metal gate. He paused, then ascended a stair, stopped, and wondered if he should say something. Again the darkness from Alexandria's window caught his attention. Now he wished that she had beaten him home. He wanted to rush to her, grab her and never let go, but she didn't know him. Did not love him. He continued on his way.

"Hello, Rellik." Her whisper stopped him mid-point on the stairwell. "That was an impressive race."

Rellik turned to her. She was leaning against the railing, her hair blowing in the cool breeze. The starry sky was captured in her eyes, and there was no sign of a smile. His heart pounded with the need to hold her.

"Hello, Alexandria," he said, descending a stair toward her.

"Alix. My friends call me Alix." She ascended one toward him.

"My apologies, Alix. I am pleased you enjoyed my victory." Rellik froze when she took another step.

"Fred and I had an interesting chat. We talked about the stakes to your race."

As she drew closer Rellik wondered what reason Fred had for betraying his trust.

"Of what particulars did he inform you?"

"He told me the loser has to leave town." Her voice peaked as if she were asking a question.

"I suspect you have a notion why." Rellik now ascended a stair for every one that she took.

"Well, considering both you and Shay asked me to the dance, I thought it might have to do with me." Alix nearly laughed when she backed him against his door.

"Your assumption is correct. Our stakes had everything to do with you. The winner has the sole right to pursue you unchallenged ... I pray you are not angered that we bargained with you as our prize." He wished he had phrased that last part differently.

"I'm more curious than angered. Why would you do such a thing? Do you love me?"

As her eyes met his, Rellik reached out and caressed her cheek....

...and that was the last time Rancour was able to bring himself to touch her. After Ariana's voice had trailed off, their eyes no longer met. They were alone in the tiny room where they slept, but it was a room for devotion no more. Now it had become a place of heartbreak. Ariana fiddled with the ring he had given her only nights ago, as her loved one packed the last of his belongings. He could not bring himself to look upon her tear-stained face, for if he dared he might forsake his honor and let love triumph. How he had come to

detest being a man of such virtue.

He slung his bundle over his shoulder and walked through the common room. Shay, sitting on a cushioned chair, gloated in triumph. Rancour gave that devil a hard glare and stormed from the cabin, wondering how the gods could have expected him to know that this merchant was the vampyre. But, reflecting back on the past few weeks, he also wondered how he could not have known.

Though the day outside had begun with a sky that drenched the Earth, by early evening the sun had broken through showering the world with drops of light. The day had turned out grand for a long journey, and for that Rancour was not at all grateful. At least if the rain had continued he could have postponed his ... banishment. His second banishment. Would he never find a place he could call "home"?

Rancour loaded his wagon and checked Storm. He heard Ariana follow him outside, and though there were birds singing, crickets chirping and a wind rustling the leaves of nearby trees, the loudest sound to him was the door she had stopped to close. For in that sound was the end of a place he had come to call "home."

Was it right to leave her with such a demon? Was that the virtue to which he clung? He loved her pure and true, knowing that she loved in him the honor he could never forsake. But what was honor if it did not complete love? Pulling himself onto the riding bench he took the steering ropes in hand. He did not look down at her, not even when she spoke to him.

"At least tell me why it is you must leave," she said.

"I made a bargain with that devil that if he bested me I'd leave town." Rancour gave in to his need to look at her and knew he could not go. But how could he consider himself a man of principle, if he broke this promise? Should he surrender to sin, his soul would never find redemption. But was hell worse than a lifetime without Ariana? "You could come with me," he said.

As she stared into his soul her shoulders slumped and she shook. Her tears stopped when she looked back at the cabin.

"I cannot leave my home."

"Ariana, me love," Rancour said tenderly to beseech her. He wanted, nay needed, to spend every moment of his life with her and, perhaps if they did so together, they could turn Shay's curse into a blessing. "This place is where you lost your family. 'Tis a place best forgotten. Come. Begin a new life with me."

Ariana bit her lower lip and brushed her hair from her eyes. Rancour noticed that their red rims looked like two sunsets, each one a sign of an end. He knew she didn't wish to leave, but he also knew she needed him as much as he her. She no longer met his emerald eyes, and reluctantly she climbed onto the riding-bench next to him. Ariana caressed his hands with her tender touch and said, "This is also the place where we met."

Rancour brought her close, kissed her forehead and caressed her cheek. "And our true love should not be coupled in a place of sorrow. We did not, after all, meet under the best of circumstance. Come with me, Ariana."

Their souls embraced in a passionate touch, and the love between them grew until separation was impossible. They knew, short of death itself, nothing would ever cause them to part.

"And would you love me forever, Rancour the Wulfsign?"

"I have never loved anyone but you," Rellik replied to Alix, who trembled at his very words.

She didn't understand why she felt so much love when they hardly knew one another. As well, she remembered how he had been only days earlier when he'd fought Derrick, when he showed up for the job interview, when he'd kicked Kharl at Icy Shakes. He had seemed so frightful to her, and yet she now felt equally drawn to him. It was as if she had known him years and not days, as if they were meeting again rather than for the first time. Her mind told her this was wrong, but her heart told her otherwise. She listened to her heart, and accepted that this feeling was right. That he was right.

"I love you," Alix whispered in his ear.

Rellik brought her close, kissed her, and opened the door to his loft. As he backed inside she stopped him.

"I don't want to have sex," she said, unable to look at him.

He caressed her chin and brought her eyes to meet his. Smiling he said, "Nor do I."

"You don't?"

"No. It would not be in my honor to bed a woman who is not my wife. Outdated and old-fashioned perhaps, but right nonetheless."

"Will you still hold me?"

"That I will."

"All night?"

"Forever," and as the word left his lips tears welled in him.

And fell. One by one. Each for every day they had spent apart.

• • •

As Fred strolled down a dark, lonely street, analyzed the events of the last few days. What he couldn't figure out was what connection all this had with Rellik. *What if you knew someone so vile … and were helpless to stop it.*

Fred stopped in his tracks and breathed the cool, thick air that had suddenly descended from a cloudless sky. A thick, bluish fog crept nearer as he recalled what Alix had told him of her dream, a nightmare he had told her just to dismiss. His heart raced, and deciding it best to keep moving, he hurried home while piecing his thoughts together.

Mostly, he wondered why Alix had never mentioned Betty's disappearance. At first he believed she worried about his feelings, after all she knew how he felt about her, but too much time had passed now. She seemed to have forgotten her best friend even existed. He sighed, so lost in thought that he didn't notice the bluish fog as it seeped in around him.

And then, the pieces began falling into place. The resounding thump of each one landing in its place knocked him from his reverie. Hypnosis … Alix's dream of a fog-creature … The bodies killed by a wolf … Shay Jackson is a vampire! And what of the wolf in Alix's dream? Who was the canine that killed the blood-drained corpses? That was the connection Rellik had with Shay.

Rellik Faolchú was a werewolf.

That was their power-struggle. Shay must have been turning the town into vampires, and Rellik was killing them … but why would he kill them? Of course, he still wasn't certain what Alix had to do with things … perhaps she was going to be Shay's next victim?

Fred now accepted that Betty had to be the unidentified corpse. Even though no police reports acknowledged his newfound suspicion, he accepted this was the most logical of choices in such an illogical situation. Shay must have repressed Alix's memory of Betty and of what had happened to her. Somehow, together, he and Alix would recall it and they would work on ending this evil. If only he could have figured things out before Shay had killed Betty.

Sometimes life just wasn't fair.

"I wish I could meet with you again, Shay!" Fred shouted at the night.

"Some wishes come true," a voice whispered, seemingly coming from the night air.

Fred froze in his tracks. He scanned the empty street, and knew whereof the voice had come. Even as he tried to make one last ditch effort to run home, he knew what fate his future held in store for him.

"My God," Fred thought as the sky rained down streaks of green and pink, and the ground swirled around him in a blue fog.

CHAPTER 15

"There is a code among the Wulfsign that commands us not to murder, unless we are challenged or we catch our enemy in an act of evil. But, I have found, that if we truly wish to see evil, we need look no further than our own hearts.

"Only ignorant people believe they can overcome evil by ignoring that sin which resides in themselves. For the only true difference between the evil that resides in another and what is in ourselves is that we have the power to change our hearts.

"What mortals do not understand is that we are like them. There are those of us who let sin become predominant, but they do not outnumber those who let virtue triumph.

"What separates us from mortals is our curse of eternal life on Earth.

"And it is a curse."

                                              —Wulfsign

Alix woke and found herself trapped inside her room. She clung to her blankets, examined the darkness and saw only the dreaded opaque orb on its ivory pedestal. Pressing her body against her headboard she recoiled when it melted into the wall, but she still chose that clammy touch over the apparitions in the sphere.

Alix prayed the horrific voice wouldn't come, knowing that once the dream ended the nightmare would begin.

"Look into the orb," the voice echoed, its mockery bringing her to weep.

"Why do you do this to me?" she screamed at the darkness as the mattress beneath her fused into the floor. "Why me?"

Alix pressed herself into a corner, but the walls shrunk around her. As she slid toward the globe, she pressed her hands and feet against the floor to stop herself, but her efforts were of no use. The pedestal bent at its elbow and reached out to her, beckoning with its bony index finger for her to peek inside.

Alix stiffened her upper lip, held her head high and not only did she look inside but she also grasped it. The fingers on the pedestal interlocked with hers and caressed her hand. The touch felt familiar, almost comforting, but the hollow echo of its raspy voice reminded her that it held the Devil's eye.

With a deep breath she peered in.

The opaque substance cleared and manifested into a crystalline movie clip of a dark, lonely street. Minnow Avenue. Near Fred's home. Alix's heart thumped so madly that she thought it might leap from her chest and take the orb's place upon the pedestal. She forced herself to look upon the apparition. The bluish fog fed on a corpse like an animal, but whomever it ate she could not tell. This time it was visible, but far too mutilated to identify.

The hand on the pedestal, no longer caressing her, released her fingers and started to rise. It took away the crystal eye so that whatever happened next she wouldn't see, but Alix held it in place. The vice released its grip over her mind, and the mental block she suffered came to an end. She now recalled the dream that had shown her Betty's demise, and knew that someone had cast a spell over her. She wondered who had such power.

The arm-pedestal allowed her to take the crystal from it, and then it reached out to hold her. Alix did not pull away, but instead let it comfort her.

"*Do not look into the orb,*" the raspy voice said this time, no longer sounding so dark.

When Alix turned her gaze back to the movie clip, she watched the fog, having finished its feast, manifest into a man. A shadow over his face hid his identity, but Alix knew who he was. Her cheeks burned nearly as bright as the blood with which he used to write a message upon the ground. He scribbled it in a strange tongue, but she somehow knew it said: "*Midnight,*" "*graveyard,*" "*tomorrow,*" and lastly, "*Wulfsign.*" Alix made a special point to memorize the message.

When the man left the scene he made no effort to

conceal his identity. He looked up at her as if he knew she watched. His smile showed the pride he took in exhibiting his actions.

Alix cursed aloud as she watched Shay strut away, as if he enjoyed ruining her life.

Then she woke.

Alix relaxed. The display on her clock read 6:15 am, only a couple of hours since she returned to her room. As dawn broke through her open window the melodies of songbirds from the birdhouse her father had built onto the gazebo danced in her ears, and the chill wind blew into her room. She pulled her comforter closer around herself.

She sank deep into her mattress and battled her anger with thoughts of her magical time with Rellik. They had cuddled in his loft on wooden crates that he used as a make-shift bed. She had tried to persuade him to come into her bedroom, but he had thought it "imprudent" with her father in the adjoining room.

"It would not be principled to insult a man in that way," he had said to her. His principles had made her laugh and love him that much more. It wasn't only the love they had found that she thought about, it was also the tears she had seen leave his dark emerald eyes. They made him seem somehow vulnerable. The patter of his rhythmic heartbeat had made her smile.

"Do you want to hear something weird?" she had asked.

He'd kissed her and smiled, the tender touch masking his raspy growl that once made her fear him. "I will listen to whatever you wish to tell me."

"Well, I've been having these flashes. Kind of like blackouts, I guess. It's like I'm another person and I've met this man." She rolled away and stared at the wall, snuggling close and holding his hand in hers. "He looks just like you."

"How flattering." He sighed and kissed the nape of her neck. She turned to him, and when their eyes met he caressed her cheek. "Are you afraid that what you feel is false?"

"No."

"Then what is it, I pray you will tell me?"

"Y'know, there's so much to you, and yet I know nothing about you."

"What would you like to know?"

"Where you come from, who your family is," she paused, and then whispered: "how you know Shay."

"I was born in Ireland. My family … well, they are dead."

"I'm sorry."

"There is no need to be; we were not close. As for Shay, I guess you could say we were rivals once. To him, your heart was but a game."

"And to you?"

He paused and rose from the bed. Alix sat, watching him rummage through his belongings. He took out a palm-sized intricately carved wooden box and walked back to her.

"You say you loved me before we met. Then you should believe that I came to you by following an ache in my heart. Only when I am with you does that pain heal."

He opened the box and took out a leather ring. "I want you to wear this, but only when you feel your soul ache for me as mine does for you."

Alix kissed him, but put the ring into her pocket. His eyes turned sad and she said, "I do love you, but things don't seem ... I don't know ... complete. I want to wear it, but only when things feel complete."

How she would treasure that memory. Rellik cared for her so much, and she as much for him. But as her thoughts returned to her nightmare, or rather to the message scribbled in blood, she wondered what she planned to do. And whether she should tell Rellik about it.

• • •

The Wulfsign stood poised over the sink as if he might be sick. He hadn't slept since Alix left, and grabbing the sink by its edges, he glared into the broken mirror. He scowled into the looking glass, not at his reflection but past it, and growled low.

Rancour ascended the steep hill, sniffing the scent of venison cooking. He knew it was from a meal Indigo prepared, undoubtedly not the last of the day, and when he neared the crest he saw he was, indeed, correct. His friend was sitting before a dying fire looking at a well roasted leg of deer.

"Indigo!" Rancour yelled to divert his tutor's attention from the food.

"You are late!"

Rancour ran to sit beside him, and rising to one knee, he grabbed him by both shoulders. First he said nothing, but then: "I know who the vampyre is!"

"Shay Jackson, your merchant friend," Indigo replied nonchalantly, catching his pupil off-guard. "You forget. I know your future.

It was, after all, my past."

"Then we can kill 'im! 'e fought me in mortal combat!"

"You did not challenge him?" The question sounded rhetorical, as though he knew. The tutor shook Rancour's grip from his shoulders and took the burning meat from the fire. "Even if you hadn't, he is a vampyre. Shay is bound by no code of honor. You, however, can murder only if you catch him in an act of evil, or are challenged."

Rancour rose, slowly, and walked to the hut. He leaned against the door, rubbed his stubbled chin, and whispered, "What do I do?"

"I don't know. My intent was never to prepare you for the vampyre."

"Then who?"

"For another who shall come."

"You told me you were vampyre hunting when you came to me!"

"Only to gain your attention. What am I to say, Rancour? Would you rather that I left you be and never came? That can be arranged. I am here for guilt and nothing more. In my view, this is the first time we have met. I do not know you well enough to care a thing about you. Should you tell me that guilt will never turn to friendship I will go."

"You 'ave been a great friend. I only wish you 'ad warned me. After all, should you wish, I would tell you o' your fate."

"I know my fate."

"You know that because you come to train me you will die?"

"Yes. And I will not change my future. Would you change yours?"

"Nay...."

"Then learn this final lesson, Rancour. This is the most important: when a human shares love with a Wulfsign, she will be reborn *one millennium after her first birth. Should that love be rekindled, both mortal and immortal will grow old and die together."*

Rancour stood before his teacher, uncertain what to say. Indeed, his life had made a turn for the better as the future held in store for him Ariana's love. But what about Indigo? What about his future that would end in such pain?

"'ow will I ever repay you?"

"By forgiving me, Rancour the Wulfsign. By forgiving me."

"Damn you, Shay," Rellik growled with hatred. "Damn you for making my life hell."

CHAPTER 16

"When mortals say they wish to go back in time to
do an event over, they assume that to do it a second
time they would not repeat the same mistake.
"What they do not consider is that to erase that
mistake is to erase that lesson it invoked, and thus
more mistakes will follow.
"If I could go back in time to do an event over,
I would go back to the best time in my life. And
rather than change it, I would savor it."

—Wulfsign

Rellik was glad that Friday night had finally come. He hated this "school" business, and sighed with relief that he would no longer have to put up a front. But without an education, what kind of mortal life could he offer Alix? He laughed, hearing Indigo's words ramble within his head. How he missed that man's friendship, and how he yearned to go to the Indigo of today to tell him about the man he would one day become. Yet, that was one thing he could never do.

Rellik paced back and forth in his loft. He hoped the patter his steps made would not draw attention from Alix or her father. Beside a half-finished portrait rested his Wulfsign sword; its metal hilt shimmering as if it called for him to wield it. He recalled the Alsandair blade he'd owned before it, the men he'd killed with it, and the hatred in himself for yielding to it.

He grabbed the weapon by its hilt and raised it to his nose. Closing his eyes he breathed the scent of death, and slowly slid it from its sheath. He held it with both hands, bent one elbow slightly more than the other, clenched his teeth and bared them, growling low and throaty. His eyes turned crimson as he thought of the lessons taught by his evil clan. They returned like thunder, as if the centuries spent forgetting were just ignorant denial.

He dropped it and let it clang, no longer caring whom he might disturb. He buried his face in his palms, shedding tears because of how hopeless, not helpless, he felt at stopping Shay's evil. He considered how much Rancour hated men who cried, and he realized he was no longer that person. "Rellik Faolchú" did not fight every challenge offered, but rather he sought for a way to resolve it peacefully. Perhaps it was the vampires he had spent most of the last millennium training with that had given him this trait. They were different from Shay, because they spoke about philosophy and values. But they were still vampires, Rellik reminded himself as he thought about them. Principled or not, vampires always gave in to their innermost selfish needs.

His mind returned to the symbols found at the previous night's murder-scene that authorities had somehow missed. *"Meán oíche"*, *"reilig"*, *"arú amárach"*, and *"Wulfsign"*. Rellik concluded, even if it made him no better than Shay, he would meet the challenge and avenge Fred. He wrapped the sword in a tarp and left for the school. He had to hurry to hide the blade in his locker if he was going to be on time to accompany Alix to her dance.

It was too bad he'd have to leave early.

Alix examined herself in the mirror to see if the new blue dress she had bought was as lovely a fit at home as it was at the store. She knew it was missing only one thing and she solved that by tying a blue ribbon that her mother had given her into her hair.

Too often tears had unexpectedly streamed down her cheeks smudging all the make-up she wore, and so she decided it best not to wear any. It was hard not to think of the loved ones she had lost: her mother, Betty and now Fred.

She knew Fred was among the dead. She knew it had been him she had seen in her dream, and she knew that Shay was responsible. She planned to meet the challenge at the graveyard with her father's loaded shotgun.

Rellik would just have to understand her having to leave the dance early.

CHAPTER 17

"Religion always seems to boil down to one thing: finding peace within oneself. But how can man find peace knowing that tomorrow may be his last, or that even this very moment may be his final one upon this world?

"Is this futile search for peace drawn from his fear of death? Does mankind truly believe that by having simply lived well that he can one day die without regret?

"As one who will always see another tomorrow, as one who knows this moment is simply a prelude to the next, I have learnt this: although those who live with principle may find heaven when they die, it is those who live without principle that find Hell on Earth."

                                                 –Wulfsign

ꭱ ven with all the strange happenings over the past
week, the dance still had a great turnout. Buses brought
in teens from schools all around the prairies, and since very
few were from Minitaw not many felt affected by the deaths
of the past few days.

Alix and Rellik stood beside a wall, watching the dance
take place without them. Alix said, "This seemed like a much
better idea on Tuesday." She pulled Rellik close.

"I apologize that my presence has driven your friends
away."

"Don't. We weren't getting along anyway. I sure wish
Fred was here."

"As do I," Rellik growled, "but it looks as though we
have company of a different sort."

Alix glanced over her shoulder and saw Kim walking
toward them with her brother.

"Hey, Blondie, why didn't you tell me you were
coming?"

"Last minute plans."

"Well, come on, girl, we're missing the dance!"

Kim grabbed Alix's arm and pulled her to the floor
where they joined a group of girls. Rellik, still snug against
the wall, kept his eyes locked on her.

"What is it about this music that makes people act as if

they are possessed?" he asked. Alix caught him watching and moved her slender body in such a way that it aroused him. "Perhaps I can see its appeal."

"That giant guy's the killer, isn't he?" Derrick asked. "You've been trying to stop him from killing people."

Rellik refused to look at Derrick. After a long moment he turned to face the native with fiery eyes. When he started to speak, a low growl emanated from his throat.

"It isn't that simple."

"You aren't a murderer, right?"

"Do you ask simply because I am not the same? I am what I am by birth, just as you are what you are by birth. There is no more truth to the legends surrounding my kind than those that surround yours. I would think that you, above anyone, would understand that."

"I won't tell anyone. But only because I owe you my life."

"You desire peace as much as I. But you are lost in an age old battle that can be won," Rellik said.

"What do you know about it!" Derrick turned on him and shouted.

Rellik stepped forward and immediately Derrick backed off.

"Because I live it every day! The difference between you and me is that you have the chance to bring peace to your people." He turned away and added, "But do you have the courage?"

"What do you know of courage? With your power you don't need to be afraid."

"I must hide! You could do anything, even become Chief if you wished."

"Who would vote for me?"

"I would vote for any man dedicated to peace. A shame we are not of the same clan."

"It's a little strange, knowing ... you know."

"What I am? Is that more important than who I am?"

"No, and that's why I'm here. I want you to know that if you need a friend, you got one."

Rellik smiled. "Thank you."

The music slowed and a softer, slower song played. The girls on the dance floor all broke away from one another, snagging guys who stood along the walls. Rellik was thankful for the relief to his ears, but when Alix approached smiling he wondered why. He hoped she didn't intend to ask him to dance. She wrapped her arms around him and he looked at the clock. It was eleven-fifteen.

"Want to dance?" She kissed his trembling lips.

"I cannot ... I have never." Rellik closed his eyes and held her to him.

"Then let me teach you. Just sway and move your feet." She moved him out to the dance floor. "You're doing it."

Rellik never wanted to let her go. He wondered if he should tell her about Shay, but feared it would give away his secret. When he held her closer, and she looked into his emerald eyes, he knew that she sensed something was wrong. She caressed his lips with her fingers.

Rellik stared deeply into her eyes and....

...after saying good-bye to his mentor and friend Rancour left the place where his clandestine lessons of shape-shifting had been taking place. He already missed the thought of coming to these

woods to speak with Indigo, and he paused a moment to take one last breath of the pollen-laden wind.

In that breath he reflected on how selfless Indigo had been to forsake his own immortality to aid him in his. He wondered what his tutor had meant by desiring forgiveness. But more so he thought about his final lesson. Why would Indigo find it so important to tell him that Ariana would return on her thousandth birthday? She was young yet and would live at least a few decades more. Why then would that be more important than how to kill a vampyre?

Rancour opened his eyes and broke into a run. He rushed back to where he had left Ariana with the wagon, praying for her safety and cursing himself for ever leaving her alone!

"You are my prayer answered," Rellik whispered into her ear. Holding her close he breathed the scent of perfume in much the same way he had that of the woods so long ago. The last few days had seemed as long as the past millennium, and Rellik was thankful for this miracle.

"You'll love me forever?" she asked.

"I'll love you even when forever ends."

"I have to go, to make sure that Sam is okay," Alix said to him as she rested her head on his chest.

Rellik half-smiled and listened to her heart beat fast. He knew she was lying, but didn't know why. He glanced at the clock and saw that it was nearly midnight, and time was at hand to meet Shay. He wanted to end this war with the creature whose heart knows only evil, and so he ignored her lie.

"We will meet up later?" she asked him, her voice prompting him for an answer.

"Yes. We will meet up tonight, in my loft."

Alix broke away from him and gave him a kiss before she walked out of the gym.

Rancour waited until he was sure she was gone before running to his locker for his sword. Once he was away from the school and out of sight, he slipped into wolf-form and headed for the graveyard.

The events of the past few days compounded in Alix's thoughts, creating an unbearable weight. She had hoped the crisp, heavy air outside might calm her busy mind, but rather than relax her the night seemed to be a partner in creating confusion. She walked towards home, thinking about Sam's rifle above the mantle. *Am I ready to kill Shay?*

Alix reached into her purse and searched for the ring. *I have never loved anyone but you,* he had told her. She bit her lip, sighed and knew by the way her heart needed him that what he had said was true. She placed the ring back into her purse. More than anything, she needed the chance at a happy life with him – and that could not happen without vengeance for the death of her friends.

Opening the door to her home, Alix did not notice a rusted late model Chevy van parked in front.

CHAPTER 18

he full moon stared down upon the graveyard from high above, calling out to his brothers, the stars, so that they, too, might rejoice in this battle of the sky. A tapestry of Northern Lights joined the celestial dominion, and together the active night unclothed much light.

Shay Jackson, sitting atop the crypt marked "Whittaker Orphans," was the only living creature in the gravesite. He captured in his eyes a promise of death, a look so stern that not even a sudden brisk wind swayed him from his post. Nor did the scent of a white dire wolf as it ran up the northern slope.

He waited patiently, keeping his back to the canine as it transformed into Rellik Faolchú. Shay waved his hands and ignited lamps around the graveyard with a single thought.

The Wulfsign stood no more than a few feet away, and his angry growls alone should have made the vamp feel supreme.

But Shay felt as if he'd lost. He turned to mist, surrounded the wagon where Rancour held Ariana, and was unsure why he'd stayed to watch. He'd destroyed Ariana, the one thing in life the Wulfsign cherished most. Or rather, he'd cursed that one thing.

Ariana opened her eyes wide enough that they threatened to swallow whatever they beheld. She screamed as her two eye-teeth grew into long fangs and her once dark complexion bled away all its color.

"What has happened to me?" she cried.

Rancour held her to him and wept. He stroked her long hair, smelled her perfumed skin and kissed her cheek.

"I still love you," he whispered.

She pushed him back. Her eyes looked empty, and goose pimples spread over her skin. "I ... feel ... hungry..." she told him. But he held her tightly and would not let go.

"We will find a cure, Ariana, we will!"

"For what? I feel alive for the first time!" She smiled and shoved him hard, sending him flying back onto the floor of the wagon. "And you, my love, will be my first meal!"

As Ariana flew at him, Rancour broke a long stake from the wooden wagon. "Would you kill me, the man you love?"

At that moment Rancour knew that if he did not kill her she would live her life as a demon. If he killed her out of mercy, and not hatred, it was not murder. It was within his honor as a Wulfsign to do so.

When she was upon him he grabbed her throat and held the weapon against her chest.

"Forgive me," he whispered, and plunged it through her heart.

And then Shay watched the Wulfsign defeat him. Not one tear left Rancour's dark, sunken eyes and the vampyre now understood what it was that this werewulf treasured most: honor. He had assumed it was love, that the woman was his world, but he was wrong. Unless he made Rancour betray his principles he would never best him. If only he'd known, it could have been so easy.

But how could he get the werewulf to challenge him senselessly, for vengeance and not for honor? How could the vampyre get him to say....

"Let's end this Shay," Rellik growled, plunging his sword into the Earth. "I know you killed Fred, and I know you killed the others. Now I'm going to send you to hell!"

"Will you now?" Shay turned to him, his face disfigured with long, pointy teeth. "You still think you can kill me?"

"That I do. I have lived among your kind and have learned your weaknesses."

"You have *hid* among them," Shay spat.

"I have spent a thousand years undoing your corruption. Not once have I ever fled from your bane."

"You should have. You should have taken your mortal and run as far and as fast as you could. After this battle I will be free to bring her into my world. She will not find you in heaven; she shall be stuck here on earth! Do you never learn?"

Shay jumped from the crypt and marched to his enemy.

"Then so shall it be. A fight to the death," the vamp said, spreading his arms in invitation.

• • •

Alix's head hurt. She walked down the hall toward the kitchen, flicked on lights as she went, and heard Sam in his den. She considered going inside, but if she found him drunk she was in no shape to handle it. *The Rifle.* This single thought came into her mind.

"Alexandria, can you come in here?" her father called from his den.

Alix complied without putting any thought into it. She walked into the den and found Sam sitting at his desk chair.

Tied up. Two men stood on either side of him, one with a pistol like the ones police use in movies, and the other a double-barrel shotgun as well as a crossbow.

"Greetings," the short rotund man said. "I am Indigo, and this is my associate Bruce Anterion."

Alix braced herself against a wall for support as the whole world spun.

"Do you want to save thousands?" the one named Bruce asked, pointing the double barrel shotgun at her while keeping his crossbow poised on Sam.

The clock struck midnight as Indigo pushed the barrel away from her.

"Now, now, Bruce. No need to be rude. Keep the gun on her father. I'm certain she'll tell us whatever we want."

"But I don't know anything." Her knees knocked, and barely able to hold herself up, Alix repeated herself, this time so softly that no one heard.

Indigo took his pistol away from Sam and clicked on the safety. He smiled and meandered toward her, reaching out his arms as if to offer a hug. Alix shrank from him, but he embraced her forcibly, and when she started crying, he offered his shoulder.

"There, there, my dear. We don't want to hurt either of you. We just want to know where your boyfriend is this fine night."

Alix lifted her head and looked into the man's eyes. Then she looked at Bruce and saw that he no longer held his menacing weapons against Sam, but an open bottle of whiskey. Her tears flowed more easily, and she wondered what to do. These men must be animals to threaten his rehabilitation; he had managed to stay sober for five whole days! Five days longer than ever before in his life.

And then it hit her. What she had to do.

"The graveyard. He's at the graveyard," Alix sobbed.

"Bruce, leave," Indigo said coldly, letting her go. Then to her father: "You should be proud to have a daughter who loves you so much. It will be a shame if after this night you return to the drink after all."

Alix watched her father's face turning red, and as Bruce ran out the front door, she felt a tinge of satisfaction.

After all, Shay was the one at the graveyard, not Rellik.

• • •

Rellik had trained for this moment for nearly a whole millennium. He threw a round-house punch, but Shay ducked and jabbed his opponent's chest. The Wulfsign fell back and felt a fist slam across his face and a back-hand against his temple.

"I have spent the last thousand years training as well," Shay said and spin-kicked his adversary's stomach. The werewolf stumbled back and brought his fists up.

"Then we fight a fair duel at last."

Shay jabbed, and Rellik ducked. The Wulfsign kicked the vamp's chest and grabbed the back of his hair, slamming his opponent's head into his knee. The vamp launched an uppercut but when he tried a back-fist the Wulfsign caught his arm and twisted him into a headlock.

"What will you do now as I snap your neck? That will take a few days to heal," Rellik said.

His opponent turned to fog. Rellik fell into a foot sweep

and tripped the vamp, and then he leaped back to his feet. He glared hard at his shocked opponent.

"I have also learned much this past millennium," the Wulfsign said with an iron voice. "I discovered you can only transform one body part to fog at a time." He couldn't stop smiling and hoped his other lessons would prove just as true. "Now get up and see what else I know."

Shay turned every body part to fog, starting with his head and ending with his feet. The eerie blue mist rose as one beast, parts of it manifesting into two clawed hands and a jaw of jagged teeth. It struck, one hand slicing Rellik's cheek but the Wulfsign caught the other, snapped the talons off, and followed the move with an elbow strike that shattered its teeth.

The fog howled and slunk away.

The vamp slowly gathered to form its human shape and turned its back on Rellik. Shay slumped, unable to rise past his knees. The Wulfsign glared, his emerald eyes burned.

"I learned something else, Shay. Whatever you attack with, it cannot be turned to fog."

Shay lay helplessly on the ground, clutching his broken hand against his chest and blood pouring from his mouth. He laughed, the apparent fear in his eyes not heard in his voice.

Rellik growled, "What is so funny?"

"My victory is turning you against your principles. I have already won."

"Then I will be your final triumph. For you, forever ends tonight. *Are you ready to become mortal?*"

Shay spun and sliced Rellik's chest, but suddenly he

stopped. The Wulfsign stared into the vamp's horrified face, uncertain what had made him halt so abruptly. He looked down and saw....

A wooden shaft that resembled a bolt from a crossbow stuck directly through his enemy's heart.

• • •

Indigo glanced at his watch, tapped it and nodded. He glared at Alix and untied Sam, then walked to the doorway. He stopped as if to savor the moment, and when he turned back his eyes looked like two endless pits. His smile was wide and bright.

"Go to him, Alexandria," Indigo said, his eyes turning icy and hard. "I want you to suffer greatly, as will I someday."

He turned and left.

Alix stared into space, stunned from that last remark. She reached into her purse and felt the ring. This time she slipped it onto her finger, unsure why. A tear left her eye and her hand tingled. Sam leaped from his chair and ran to her. He grabbed and shook her as if to wake her.

"Alexandria! We have to go help him!"

"But, Rellik isn't there."

In the silence they threw their arms around one another. Alix sobbed, knowing she had made a terrible mistake. Both she and Sam turned to the mantel and stared at the portrait of their lost loved one.

Then at the shotgun beneath.

• • •

Rellik mentally scanned the area and prayed that the

bolt had come from a crossbow Alix operated. But as Shay fell, turning into a pillar of dust for the evil he was, Rellik's power died.

"I'm mortal," Rellik realized when all his senses lost their heightened ability. He looked up and saw a large man running at him.

"I am Bruce Tannis," the stranger growled, leaping at Rellik. "I AM SALVATION!"

The Wulfsign caught his opponent and tried pushing him away, but forgot to compensate for his lost strength. Bruce tackled him to the ground, getting on top and pummelling him with his fists. Rellik wrapped his legs beneath his adversary's waist, threw him off, and scrambled to his feet. His nose bled and one eye had started to puff out.

"Don't be a fool!" the Wulfsign shouted. "I am mortal now! If I wasn't I would have turned to a wolf and ripped out your throat."

"I was told you like sport." Bruce took out a silver laced Buckmaster. "I shall save thousands by killing you!"

Bruce swiped but Rellik dodged, caught his opponent's arm, and kicked his kneecap. Bruce staggered and yelled, but managed to pull his arm free. He tried to rise but fell back to the ground, his leg broken and unable to support him.

"I'll get you an ambulance," Rellik said as he turned to leave.

"Don't mock me," Bruce spat. "Before you kill me, at least tell me why you were fighting the vamp. Was it over the same prey? Was it the girl?"

"I was stopping him from killing anyone ever again, you fool." Rellik turned and walked to his sword. He took it from the ground and returned to the man.

"Then why did you kill the Tannises? Why did you kill my parents!"

"I saved them. I saved them all," Rellik kneeled and balanced himself with his weapon. "I am not evil. The legends of my kind are nothing but lies. You cannot become a werewolf by drinking water from my paw print, nor from eating food cooked by my hands. My bite does not spread my seed, nor does the full moon make us change. It was wrong of humans to make up those fallacies to justify their hatred. But vampires are different. They crave pleasure and spread their kind like a disease. Do you understand?"

"Yes I do." Bruce gave a shout and grabbed the sword from Rellik. With one last effort, he thrust the blade through Rellik's chest.

CHAPTER 19

Bruce staggered to his feet, using the sword as a crutch. The vampire was long dead and, though the werewolf clung desperately to life, he would soon join his counterpart.

"If silver is also a myth, fight or not, you're going to hell."

"I will die," Rellik choked on his blood, "but only because I have been made mortal. You missed my heart."

"But you didn't miss my parents' hearts."

"I saved them from a life of evil, from living as this vamp before you."

"You're a creature like them. If you aren't evil, why would they have to be?" Bruce's voice resounded with hatred.

Rellik thought about the vampires he had trained with, the renegade vamps that sought a life of principle and forgiveness. He wondered again if it was possible for a vamp to redeem himself. If so, could Ariana have also been redeemed? As he wiped away a tear that had come down his cheek he shivered from the cold.

"Vampires cannot be saved. I did not kill Ariana for nothing!"

Atop the western hill, Alix and Sam watched the strange scene in horror. As they descended the crest, Sam clung to his hunting rifle and Alix clung to him. They looked at each other, then at the man standing over Rellik. Sam did what he thought he must, knowing only that he had to save the outsider.

He pointed his gun directly at the man, closed his eyes, and pulled the trigger. It disturbed him when revenge eased his heart. His daughter cried at the sight of him killing, but as he rubbed his wrists from where the ropes had cut he knew he had done the just deed.

"Go to him. I'll call an ambulance and police," he said.

"Thank you." Alix hugged him and whispered: "Dad."

Rellik lay helplessly, but knew when he saw Alix rush to him that he could at last die in peace. She sat in the blood-stained grass, resting his weak body against hers, clutching his jacket against the wound. He embraced her and she kissed his forehead gently. Rellik knew his time had ended. The world about him grew ever colder and he wondered how he'd ever forgive Indigo for this evil. He truly wondered how his soul could ever forget this.

Rellik thought about his life. It had been long, solitary, and hardly worth the value mortals placed on theirs. In truth, he had come to terms with his immortality only because of Indigo's fellowship, and it was because he had come to terms that he had loved more deeply than any one person deserved.

The Wulfsign looked into Alix's eyes and knew that, because of her, because of a memory from so long past and yet so near, he would never regret his life. Yet he also knew, as he felt death coming closer to claim him, that her soul would live on. Perhaps even to love another ... would she forget him? *Does she remember?*

He watched her tears run freely, dropping from her trembling chin to land on his face. He smiled, ignored the pain from his wound and caressed her soft cheeks. Wiping away her sorrow he wished he could be courageous for her. He wished he could be the brave Rancour one last time, but as his eyes released sadness from them he knew he could not hide it from her.

"The ambulance is coming ... my Dad called for help," she said, but her voice died in the air between them.

Rellik still smiled. A full smile this time. His eyes, too, had lost their dark quality as the emerald color danced with light.

"It no longer matters."

"Don't be foolish." Alix fought back against the grief that was overtaking her.

"Do you remember the first time we met?"

"Of course. That day at school."

Rellik reached out to touch her lips. The look of sorrow was embedded within his emerald eyes, and when he spoke, his lips barely moved.

"*No. Do you remember the* first *time we met?*"

Alix didn't understand, but by the expression on his face this memory meant a lot. She wondered if the loss of blood had clouded his mind, but the intense look in his eyes told her that he held strong to his senses. And, what was more, that voice had come from her mind!

When she kissed his fingers he moved them to her forehead and pressed. The voice again came to her saying, *Search your dreams.*

Alix closed her eyes and became light-headed. The

pressure from his fingers released, and her head stopped spinning. When she opened her eyes she was in a small room, alone, with the crystal orb from her dreams. As in her dreams, fear gripped her.

"It was you?" she called out, but received no answer. "How could you do this to me?" But there was no voice in the room commanding her to look into the sphere. Alix knew this time it held a memory from the past instead of an image of the present, but it had become a symbol of fright and she wondered what hellish experience it might recall. Perhaps it was best to leave that what is suppressed alone.

"Do you remember the first *time we met?"* Rellik's voice had sounded so full of sorrow that Alix knew she had to see. Had he demanded her to watch those times before so she might understand, and not because he wanted to frighten her? Alix looked deeply into the globe, recalling her last dream when the pedestal had caressed and comforted her.

It didn't feel as horrific as it had before. Clouds covered the night sky like a blanket, and the there was a full moon. Droplets of water rested on the ground and trees, as a rainfall had just taken place. There was a small cottage where candlelight flickered in the windows and smoke rose from the chimney.

The night felt cold, and a young girl was walking with haste along a path that led from the cabin into sparse woods nearby. She was in her late teens, and carried an empty wooden bucket. Alix couldn't tell if she knew her as a thick fog had begun to envelop the scene.

"No! Not again," Alix whispered, covering her eyes.

"No, not again," the voice said as it had before, but now

sounding gentle, even comforting. She wondered if it had always been that way. Opening her eyes she was no longer alone in the room. She couldn't see anyone, but rather she sensed a presence giving her courage and strength.

"Fear not your own memory," the presence told her.

Alix took that encouragement and lifted her head, again staring into the orb. But the fog had grown so thick that she could see nothing. Then it grew so fast that it started pouring from the ball, and when she drowned in it she lost sense of where she was. A cold breeze rose as the clothes she wore changed into a woollen dress and shawl. The fog parted so she could look about her strange ... no, familiar ... surroundings. She had become the girl she had seen walking along the path in the woods. The girl from her story. The one for whom she could not think up a name.

Alix checked the path to see if there was a well for water to convince herself that this was her own memory. There was, and she recalled she needed water for her sick brother who was fever-stricken and needed water to cool down. Alix shivered from fright, wishing the illness hadn't taken her parents. But there wasn't much she could do without medicine.

Her father had warned her many times not to walk in the woods after dark - especially during a full moon. Just before he died he'd set wolf traps around the well to help ease her fear, and though the night had grown dark she knew where to avoid them. She clenched her bucket tightly for added courage and kept her spirits brave by reminding herself of her sibling's dire need for water. As long as she didn't falter, this wouldn't take long.

When she reached her destination Alix tied the rope to the pail and lowered it hastily down the shaft. The woods amplified every noise, and her hands shook making the task difficult. Her heart pounded as though someone were watching ... as though someone studied her every move. The well was an endless pit.

Alix was concentrating on her task, until something grabbed her. She dropped the bucket back into the deep well, screamed, and slapped her shoulder to ward off the assailant. She fell to the ground in panic, and then laughter, as she wiped off the remnants of a grasshopper from her hand. The only demons true and real were the ones in her imagination.

"Are you well, me lady?" a deep, raspy voice asked.

Alix couldn't move. Her muscles froze. She felt helpless as whoever had spoken slowly sauntered until he stared at her. He was short, brandished a very large build and wore a black hooded cloak. He carried with him no noticeable weapons, but his garment was long and bulky.

"Please don't..." Alix's voice failed, and wishing she had left the bucket out in the rain she hoped her death would be quick and painless. But as he advanced closer the sound of metal teeth slamming shut answered her prayers. She found strength in the trap that had caught him and rose to run.

But before she fled the stranger's hood fell from his face, and Alix looked into his emerald eyes. She saw nothing but the soul of a lost boy, one that had been left all alone in the world. She turned and still ran, but stopped after taking only a few strides.

Even after he had the iron jaws off his leg he had made

no attempt to pursue her. He rubbed his wound but didn't dress it, his eyes turned so sorrowful that time itself ceased in them. She saw no blood but knew that such a wound would bleed him to death. He smiled at her.

"You need not fear me. I mean you no 'arm. I will leave if me presence frightens you."

His voice, though deep and raspy, was soft and whispered. Alix ignored her fright and walked a few paces closer. His stern face looked a bit horrific, but his eyes, much like his voice, had a gentle and caring quality. When she sat near him the stranger ripped material from his cloak to bandage the wound. It still did not bleed.

She cleared her throat, and when she found control over her trembling voice she told him, "I-I need water. My brother is sick."

He still smiled, as if pleased that her fear had subsided. Alix rose to approach the well, keeping it as a barrier between them.

"Then I pray you will accept me apology, and I will be on my way." The stranger turned to face her as he knelt on the muddy ground.

His dark emerald eyes shone with loneliness and, as he turned to leave, Alix replied, "That wound will become infected. Come to the cabin. I'll treat it. I cannot offer medicine, but food and fresh linen...."

For a moment he didn't move. Then he rose and replied, "That would be kind and I thank you. I am called Rancour the Wulfsign."

He slowly stretched his open hand over the well toward her. His gesture frightened her, but as Alix felt his strong grasp this memory suddenly became completely hers. No longer an image, this recollection was now reality.

"Ariana. I am called Ariana. What brings you out into these woods?"

Rancour walked around the well and took the rope. As he lifted the heavy bucket with ease he said, "I am o' the clan Alsandair. Me clansmen are evil incarnate, but I am not. They branded me a demon for my virtue," he paused and gave her a look as though he were a child, watching his first sunset. Then he handed her the rope and said, "I am no longer o' that clan and no longer in search of battle. Now I search for acceptance, but as of yet I have found no where I can call me 'ome."

The fog again enveloped them, and as Alix woke from her dream she found herself holding the outsider whom she now loved. Again she heard a voice deep in her mind, *"Do you remember the first time we met?"*

She wept and held her love tight, replying between sobs, "Yes, Rancour. I remember."

He caressed her cheek. Alix stared into his eyes and watched the despondency he had found in this world dissolve. He smiled, and she knew that, one last time, he had become the innocent Rancour. A man unaware of the burden of immortality.

"Then I take death as a reward, and not the curse you mortals deem it as."

His heavy body turned limp in her arms and she buried her face in his long black hair. She cried, "Know that you have found your place of acceptance. Your home is my heart.

I will love you always."

And as the ambulance arrived its siren was drowned by a raspy voice in her mind: *"Then I 'ave found me 'eaven."*

"When one considers what is denied to an immortal, one often thinks of death. But what is truly denied is love.

"When I fell in love with Ariana it frightened me what she might do should I tell her of the Wulfsign. She was human, with human prejudice, and would be frightened by what she did not understand. I thought that I had hid the truth from her because I loved her, but now I know better.

"When you love someone that emotion will drive you to be honest, even when that honesty may drive you apart."

"As I write this final page in the Year of Our Lord 1005, I vow to wait for my true love to return. And when she does, I will surrender to her my immortality for the chance to love truthfully. For to me it is not so much a question if I will give up living for ever, but a blessing that I can.

"I vow that, someday, I will die and the last thing on Earth I see will be my love's tender gaze."

-Wulfsign

James McCann *is the author of three YA novels*
including Rancour *and* Pyre, *both published with*
Simply Read Books. Pyre *was given a honorable*
mention by the Ontario Library Top Ten Best Bets 2008
as well as a top pick for teens by the Vancouver Sun, 2007.
Flying Feet, *a YA novel on Mixed Martial Arts,*
was published by Orca Books in 2010.
James McCann grew up on the icy plains of Manitoba,
where he spent most of his teenage years reading comics
and playing Dungeons and Dragons. Both of these hobbies
taught him the storytelling tools that he now uses as an
author and creative writing instructor.
In 2002 he ventured to the west coast, where he's worked
as a bookseller and a workshop leader, mentoring youth in
creative writing. When he isn't writing, McCann is practicing
tae kwon do or going on hikes with his Shih Tzu, Conan.
Unlike the creatures of the night of which he writes, he lives
peacefully in the daylight.